THE SANGUINE SCROLL

JAMES E WISHER

SAND HILL PUBLISHING

CHAPTER 1

L ord of the Dead sat in his hard chair of bone and glared at the other High Lords. The eight of them— Lord Dagon's representative never left his watery realm outside the city and had no great interest in the goings- on of his earthbound cohorts—had gathered in the dark council chamber.

Since all of them could see in the dark, no one bothered to conjure a light. The entire room was decorated in black. The walls were charred by fire, onyx tile covered the floor, and the great round table was made of ebony. At each High Lord's place, a special sigil had been carved into the table and filled with melted ruby. The red markings were the only color in the room.

The subject under discussion was what to do about his wayward underling. Lady White's escape pleased no one, though he couldn't deny a certain amount of pride at his former apprentice's determination. She had always been a tough one. He very much regretted her loss, but someone had to answer for what happened in the Celestial Empire and it wasn't going to be him.

Life would be so much easier for him if Lord Astaroth would simply deny power to those that didn't follow his orders. But the demon lords didn't work that way. As long as Lady White and Marius honored Astaroth and the bargain they made with him, their lord cared nothing for who they served in the mortal realm.

The others had been going on for hours about Lord of the Dead's many supposed failings. He listened with the patience of the dead. They all acted as if this was his fault. Like Abaddon's followers hadn't been the ones to fail in their task to execute her. He hadn't summoned the outsiders that saved her then destroyed Dagon's guardian. Like the rest of them, he'd been watching the battle from a safe distance. And while the results surprised him, he certainly had no intention of taking the blame.

As he waited for a break in the litany of abuse, his glowing red gaze darted around the room to rest on Lord of Unholy Flames. Abaddon's representative had gotten his fair share of criticism earlier. But he'd already lost seven Hellfire Warlocks in the attempt to take down Lady White, a price everyone agreed was enough to make up for his part in her escape.

At last, Lord of Broken Earth, Lord Baphomet's representative, broke off his tirade and glared at Lord of the Dead. "What have you to say for yourself?"

His massive body dripped sweat and Lord of the Dead was once again reminded that lacking a sense of smell could be a blessing, especially given the company he often kept.

"What would you like me to say?" he asked. "I gave my blessing for her execution. We all agreed that it should be one of you that completed the task. That Lord of Unholy Flames' warlocks weren't up to the task is hardly my fault."

Lord of Unholy Fames leapt to his feet, the blue flames burning in his eyes flaring with his anger. Emaciated to the point of being little more than a skeleton wrapped in flesh like leather, most believed his patron had burned away everything unnecessary when he took the man as his chosen.

"You're not going to turn this back on me! My followers would have had her if the outsiders hadn't shown up when they did."

Lady of Lust, Lord Ardent Lilly's chosen representative, stood and raised her perfectly formed arms in a request for silence. If there was a more beautiful woman in the world, Lord of the Dead couldn't picture her. Shining black hair hung down to the woman's slender waist. Large, high breasts strained the fasteners of her thin red robe. Unlike most of those that followed one of the nine, the lady's glowing eyes were inviting rather than terrifying.

"My fellow lords, this bickering is pointless. The important thing now is figuring out what we're going to do next. As I see it, our options are simple. Either we send hunters after her, or we let her go and move on with our work. How say you?"

Given that they were demon worshippers, it was a given that the vote would be to hunt Lady White down. Sometimes their desire for revenge got in the way of important work, but that couldn't be helped. In the end, they were all slaves to their nature.

"We're decided then," Lady of Lust said. She turned her gaze on Lord of the Dead and for a moment the memory of a heartbeat ran through him. "Do you know where she is?"

He shook his head. "Lord Astaroth still favors her. My

inquiries have gone unanswered. If we wish to find her, we'll have to search via other means."

Lord of Broken Earth snorted and shifted in his chair, causing the stout wood to creak.

Lady of Lust turned her attention to him. "Has Lord Baphomet provided some insight to you?"

"Not as yet." He snarled and looked away.

If Lord of the Dead had still possessed lips, he would have smiled. "I will handle the search and execution of my former subordinate. As I should have done in the first place."

"You require no aid?" Lady of Lust asked.

"No." He stood and swept out of the council chamber. It was a grand, arrogant gesture, one the others wouldn't let him forget should he fail.

His personal tower sat only a short walk from the council's tower. The yellowish-white spire was made from the bones of people sacrificed to Astaroth. Far harder than stone, the demon lord's magic made it an impregnable fortress.

He made the trip in silence, his mind racing as he considered the possibilities. Despite his confident assertions, finding Lady White would be no easy task. If Astaroth's magic wouldn't provide him with the information he needed, more mundane methods would be required. Luckily, he had contacts in the world outside the Land of the Demon Binders. One of whom specialized in the collection of information.

If she couldn't get him the information he needed, then no one could.

———

L ord of the Dead entered his private casting chamber. Cold, austere stone walls devoid of decoration or lights enclosed a circle inscribed with runes. The touch of one of his familiars caressed his cheek. That slight contact would have left a black scar on an ordinary human, but he had long since moved beyond such mortal weakness. Now corruption only made him stronger.

At his command, darkness flooded the runes, pure corruption summoned straight from Astaroth's hell. In addition to binding demons, his circle served a number of other uses. Like instantaneous communication.

He snatched the familiar out of the air and ripped it in half. Its psychic scream of pain gave him a thrill of pleasure along with a burst of extra power. Corruption fed on pain along with other negative emotions and so did he. Not to the degree that the tortured freak of a Golmol worshipper Lord of Pain did, but any power was to be savored.

His mind focused on Melisandre Raven. He'd met her a decade ago when one of her merchant ships had sailed into their harbor. Sponsoring her visit had seemed risky at the time, but unlike their most recent visitors, he had profited many times over from the association.

When the woman's cold, calculating features were clear in his mind, Lord of the Dead hurled half his familiar into the circle.

Traveling through corrupt ether halfway around the world, his familiar quickly arrived at Melisandre's mansion in Port Settle. Unlike when he contacted his servants, Lord of the Dead didn't expect an instant response. To his surprise, he felt the connection only seconds later.

He threw the second half of the familiar into the circle,

completing the connection. The darkness warped into the form of an oval. In the center of it a woman's face appeared. Melisandre had high cheekbones, pale skin, dark, cold eyes, and black hair pulled back in a severe bun. No one would call her beautiful and he doubted she'd care if they did.

"Lord of the Dead," she said. "This is a welcome surprise. Can I be of some service?"

"Hopefully. One of my agents has gone rogue and I require assistance locating her."

"Of course. Good help is so hard to find. Can you tell me a little more? An indication of where she was headed perhaps?"

"She fled west on a ship bound for the new empire. The name escapes me. They should have arrived by now I think."

Melisandre nodded. "I believe I know the ship you're thinking of. It arrived in the port of Lux a few days ago. The only woman my agents saw was in her late twenties, dark hair, likely hailing from the Celestial Empire. There was also a girl in her late teens. Are either of those your wayward agent?"

Lord of the Dead raged inwardly. "No. Lady White has a very distinct appearance. And that isn't it. The ship, however, is likely the same one, as they were on their way home from the Celestial Empire. If she wasn't on board, then where is she?"

Melisandre's slender hand appeared in the image as she touched her chin. "Their course would have brought them west, along the coast of the Dead Lands. Might they have dropped her off somewhere? A member of your cult would be right at home in the Dead Lands. There is certainly something going on there."

The Dead Lands would be a perfect place for Lady White to hide. But the continent was huge. Locating one person on such a vast landmass would be nearly impossible. "What do you mean something is going on there?"

"One of my agents in the City of Coins reported that Eddred of Markane has returned and is looking to hire mercenaries to investigate the interior. He claims to have magic from Lord Valtan himself capable of protecting the group from the undead roaming the area. Despite that, he's had trouble securing a party."

That didn't surprise Lord of the Dead in the least. Though Amet Sur had vanished before Lord of the Dead rose to his current position as High Lord, he'd read everything he could find about the Arcane Lord. His ability to create undead rivaled even Astaroth's cult. Perhaps Lady White sought some secret that would allow her to take his place.

Lord of the Dead couldn't allow that. "I believe you may be right. My agent will travel to the City of Coins today. Thank you for your assistance. When next your traders arrive, they will find a warm welcome."

"Thank you, Lord of the Dead. If I may make a suggestion, I'm preparing an expedition of my own to the Dead Lands. Perhaps our agents can work together for our mutual benefit."

Lord of the Dead's suspicion perked up. "What is your interest there?"

"Eddred is searching for Amet Sur's capital. The wealth hidden there must be beyond comprehension. I want it. Or as much of it as I can get home."

Lord of the Dead considered for a moment then nodded. "Very well, my agent will meet yours in the City of Coins. He wears a ring with the symbol of Astaroth."

"Have him come to Raven Trading's warehouse on the dock. My people will be waiting to meet him."

Lord of the Dead severed the connection, destroying his

familiar in the process. A minor cost for such a useful spell. Even better, he now knew where to begin the hunt. And if there was one thing the Hound of Astaroth was good at, it was hunting.

Lord of the Dead sent his thoughts ahead of him as he strode down the tower steps toward the main gate. All was silent, as it should be. No human servants meant no light spoiled the perfect darkness of his tower. Darkness was his true home and he needed no help to see through it.

At the bottom of the stairs, an inky black shape waited. Jackal, the Hound of Astaroth, took a knee and bowed his head. "Command me, Master."

"Lady White has fled our nation and taken refuge in the Dead Lands. By the will of the council and her own failure, she was to be destroyed. Abaddon's cult failed in their task, so it has fallen to us to clean up their mess. You will find her and end her. Allies will meet you in the City of Coins. Usually, I would send you on your own, but they have access to useful information that should speed your course. Should they interfere in any way, feel free to kill them."

Jackal stood and raised his head. Handsome human features peeked out from the folds of his hood. As long as he suppressed his demonic aura, no one would guess Jackal was anything more than an especially attractive man. That's what made him such a useful servant.

"I will bring you her head, Master."

"As long as you remove it from her neck, I don't care what else you do with it. Your transport is waiting at the dock. You will find your allies at a warehouse owned by Raven Trading on the City of Coins' dock. Show them your ring, so they'll know you."

"I will not fail you, Master."

"I know you won't. There is no one else I would trust with this mission."

Jackal bowed and strode out the tower gate.

Lord of the Dead had full confidence in his hound, but Lady White was no pushover. Losing two of his most powerful subordinates would be a heavy blow to the cult. No doubt his peers hoped for exactly that.

Well, he'd be happy to disappoint them.

CHAPTER 2

The stink of the docks mingled with shouts from merchants in the air of Port Settle's market. Hundreds of stalls sprawled through the park selling everything from salted beef to magic crystals. Gareth had heard tales of the bazaar in the City of Coins. Merchants claimed you could buy anything there. He didn't know if that was true, but you could certainly get most anything here. And if you were clever and quick, you didn't have to pay for most of it.

Gareth's gaze wandered from person to person. He'd lived in the city for all of his twenty-two years and the stink no longer troubled him, but it made spotting the people from out of town easy. They were the ones crinkling their noses if they were poor or covering them with a perfumed handkerchief if they were rich.

Handkerchief people generally made better marks.

Speaking of which, there was one now. A fat pigeon just waiting to be plucked. A heavy pouch dangled from the man's belt, jingling faintly as he dickered with a silk merchant.

Gareth took two steps toward the man before turning aside. An eagle-eyed guard dressed like a common laborer was watching over everyone that came anywhere near the mark. A soft sigh slipped out. That pouch would have seen Gareth through the rest of the week and then some.

Why couldn't the guards wear a proper uniform? It was just plain sneaky keeping your muscle out of sight like that. Making them so obvious even a blind man could see them struck Gareth as more effective anyway.

But then what did he know? Gareth was a thief, not a mercenary.

His stomach growled, suggesting food might make a useful target. His stomach's larcenous thoughts aside, Gareth never stole from the food merchants. Most of them were barely scraping by. He preferred to steal from those rich enough to afford losing the coin he took. Plus, they usually had enough to make it worthwhile.

He angled across the market, dodging overburdened shoppers as he went. He still had a few silver pennies from his last job, that would cover a bowl of fish stew. After that, his options for dinner grew dim.

Rounding a bend, he froze. A pair of the merchant council's guards were hassling old lady Wren. She had to be ninety and made her living selling tools she made from the fish bones she collected along the dock. Mostly fishhooks, needles, and toothpicks. She barely made enough to keep herself fed, much less pay any sort of tax. Of all the merchants in the bazaar, why her? She had to be the sweetest, most unassuming woman he'd ever met. She even gave him sweets when he was a kid.

One of the guards slammed his fist on her rickety table, rattling the modest spread of tools on it. Gareth watched, his anger coming to a low boil. If they hurt her, he'd make them regret it.

Finally, she held up a pathetically thin purse. One of them snatched it out of her hand and they stalked off to bother someone else.

Gareth drew the black-bladed dagger he always carried and hid it along his forearm. He set out on a line to intercept the guards. When he got close, he looked to one side like someone called his name and walked right in front of them.

"Out of the way!" One of the guards shoved him to the right.

Gareth staggered, his hands going out to grab the guard to steady himself. The moment he made contact, the dagger went to work, slicing the guard's purse strings.

When the man shoved him to the ground, Gareth let himself fall. "Beg your pardon, sir. Forgive me, I was distracted."

The guards shared a disgusted look and stomped off, their swords swinging and mail clinking. Gareth waited until they were out of sight, hopped to his feet, and dusted himself off.

Easy money.

He sheathed his dagger and ambled back to old lady Wren's table. "You okay?"

She looked up at him, her face crinkling as she smiled. Had anyone ever had so many wrinkles? "Fine, dear. The guards stopped to collect my stall rent for the second time this month."

She spat through her toothless gums. That about summed up everyone's opinion of the local constabulary.

"Funny thing." Gareth pulled out the pouch he'd stolen and set it on her table. "I just ran into them and they felt so bad about cheating you, they donated this generous purse. Best not let anyone see it."

"Heaven bless you, boy." Swollen knuckles didn't slow her down when she made the purse disappear.

When her hand came back up she held a small treat wrapped in wax paper. "Taffy?"

Gareth accepted the treat and grinned. "Thanks, Mrs. Wren."

He left her stall and made his way double time out of the market. Soon enough that guard would notice his missing purse and Gareth wanted to be in another district when he did.

The walk from the market to the docks took only five minutes and was blessedly guard free. He strolled down the boardwalk, ignoring the happy couples out for a noon stroll. While he didn't begrudge them their happiness, he didn't have any great desire to observe it either. Just ahead waited his destination, a disreputable tavern that worked hard to look rundown, but was actually built like a fort.

Lucky for him and his empty money pouch, he had a friend that owed him a drink. The bartender at the Belching Mermaid had a sideline fencing stolen goods. Gareth had used his services plenty of times, even offering an extra five percent on his end for future consideration. Plenty of thieves would balk, but Gareth had learned fast that having people owe you could be more valuable than a few extra coins.

He pushed through the swinging doors and found the common room as empty as he'd hoped. Not a single one of the twenty tables had an occupant. Behind the bar, Tobias restocked the bottles seemingly unaware that Gareth had entered. Tobias's broad back and bald head made him instantly recognizable.

While the place did a fantastic business after dark, in the

early afternoon you had your choice of seats. You could also discuss less-than-legal business opportunities without fear of anyone overhearing.

Gareth had never understood why everyone assumed illegal business always happened at night. The planning, at least, was usually best accomplished in the middle of the day when no one expected it.

"What's a guy got to do to get a drink around here?"

Tobias spun, a bottle of whiskey in each hand. His face looked freshly shaved and even his eyebrows were missing.

"Gareth. And here I was hoping for a paying customer." Tobias pointed at one of the barstools. "Take a load off."

Gareth settled down. "How's business?"

"Oh, you know." Tobias placed a mug of ale in front of him. "Why, you looking for work?"

"Yeah, things are tight. Besides, I think I'd best avoid the market for a while."

Tobias laughed and poured himself a shot. "What did you do this time?"

Gareth told him then shrugged. "What choice did I have? Those bastards can't pick on an old lady and get away with it."

"A thief with a sense of honor. I always said you were crazy. Depending on how crazy, I might just have a lead for you."

"I'm all ears."

———

After dark, the streets of the merchant quarter were nearly silent. Certainly Gareth did little to break the hush. The biggest trick was avoiding the magical lights situated every twenty paces. Years of practice made it easy for him, almost like dancing. They were far enough inland that you couldn't smell the docks unless the wind was blowing from the wrong direction.

Mansions surrounded by iron fences sprawled here and there while smaller homes filled in the gaps. Even the more modest buildings would have housed half a dozen families from Gareth's neighborhood with ease. He currently lived in a one-room garret on the fourth floor of a disreputable tenement.

Of course, if Tobias's tip paid off, he might be able to upgrade his living situation. But that was a big if.

According to the bartender, one of the merchant council members, Melisandre Raven herself, had recently received a delivery. Servant gossip said it was a small statuette made of solid mithril. More likely it was silver. In this neck of the woods, mithril was harder to come by than morals. Not that there was an oversupply of the latter. Even if it was silver, a couple pounds would bring him enough coin to last three months at least, maybe four if he was careful.

A faint jingle alerted him to an approaching patrol.

Gareth ducked into an alley and crouched behind a metal garbage box. At least the quiet made it easy to hear the guards coming. While far from the most diligent of guardians, they at least knew enough not to talk while out on patrol.

The pair went rattling on by and he waited until the clinking moved beyond his hearing to emerge onto the street. A quick look left and right revealed nothing to concern him. The guards were so overconfident in this part of the city it almost made sneaking in too easy.

Almost. Gareth never complained when a job was too easy. Only idiots strutted around claiming to want a real challenge. A real challenge was apt to see you dead or in a jail cell. Unimpressive as his little garret was, he had no desire to trade it for a stone cell.

He reached the wall surrounding Raven Manor and paused to consider. It was a proper wall too. Solid stone and twenty feet tall. Far more impressive than the iron fences the other merchants used.

That said, the wall was rough, with plenty of hand- and toeholds. Climbing shouldn't be a problem. What would be was knowing what waited on the other side. Ending up in the lap of a guard would end his night in a hurry.

Gareth shrugged, pulled on his thin leather gloves, and started climbing. At the top he chinned himself up and had a look at the grounds. Glass crunched under his hands, making him extra glad he brought his gloves. Beyond the wall waited nothing but open lawn. There were no shrubs to hide behind, no statues, no nothing. At least there were no lights, beyond the stars and a quarter moon.

Quick and quiet, working mostly by feel, he topped the wall and started down the opposite side. At the base he paused and listened for any sign that his entrance had been noticed. After a full five minutes he decided that it hadn't and snuck away from the wall.

Stealth was pointless with nowhere to hide.

Gareth went for speed.

He sprinted across the open ground, skidding to a stop beside a closed door.

Once more he stopped and listened for five heart-pounding minutes.

Still no sign of guards. In the back of his mind, doubt nibbled. There had to be mercenaries around here somewhere. All the rich and powerful had private armies at their beck and call. He seriously doubted the richest and most powerful of all didn't.

Should he bolt or did he keep going?

As usual, greed won out over good sense. That statuette, whatever it was made of, would keep him flush for months. No way were a few bad vibes going to stop him.

He tried the handle but of course it was locked.

Crouching, he pulled two stiff wires from a pouch in his pocket and got to work. After a bit of teasing, the tumblers fell into place and he twisted the lock open. The inside of the mansion was even darker than the outside. Lucky for Gareth, he'd always had good night vision.

On both sides of the entry hall, paintings were firmly affixed to the wall. Not that he had any intention of trying to steal a painting half as tall as he was. Gareth preferred his loot a bit more portable.

Quiet as a summer breeze, he snuck through the halls. Once again, not a guard or servant or anything. He was getting a bad case of the willies. The sooner he found the statue and split, the better. According to Tobias, the statue was on display in some kind of private museum, happily on the ground floor.

He passed through a dining room bigger than his entire apartment, a living room with a huge fireplace filled with dying embers, and a library with more books than he'd ever seen in one place.

At last, he came to another locked door. This had to be it. He was running out of rooms to check.

He knelt and looked the lock over. The picks came out next and he got to work. Immediately he felt something that shouldn't be there, a thin wire that had nothing to do with the actual mechanism. That had the feel of a trap. He felt oddly better. Finally, some security.

Not particularly good security, but something.

Gareth moved off to one side and pressed the wire.

A dart shot out, passing through the space he'd just occupied. The spring hadn't made much noise, but in the dark, silent house, it sounded like an explosion. A few more wiggles confirmed that it was a single shot. He'd seen designs with up to four darts in the magazine.

Satisfied that the door was safe, he picked the lock and pushed it open on silent hinges. Dozens of stands filled the room, each holding something rare and valuable. The statuette was supposed to be the centerpiece.

He snuck across the room, quiet as a mouse. When he reached the halfway point, a blinding light filled the room.

Dazzled, he threw an arm across his eyes.

The familiar jingle of mail came from every direction.

Gareth really didn't want to lower his arm, but pretending if he couldn't see them, the mercenaries couldn't see him wouldn't accomplish much.

Finally, he lowered his arm and sighed. Fourteen guards, all armed with loaded crossbows, had him surrounded.

He grimaced and raised his hands. "Okay, you caught me. What happens now?

Hopefully not him getting dragged to a room with an easy-to-clean stone floor and having his throat cut.

"Now we have a chat," a voice from above said.

Gareth gazed up at the source of the voice. A stern, harsh-looking woman with cold eyes and long dark hair stood on a second-floor balcony overlooking the museum. Though he'd never seen her before, he was pretty sure she was the lady of the house, Melisandre Raven.

"About what?" he asked.

"A job. Bring him."

The guards were none too gentle bringing him. They searched him everywhere, including places that should never be searched. Next they relieved him of his dagger and tools. Not that he was dumb enough to try anything, but he would have felt better if they'd allowed him to retain his gear.

At last they half dragged him to a side room that appeared designed for conducting interviews. Melisandre waited, seated behind a plain, empty desk. Gareth was thrust into the empty chair in front of her. His possessions were placed on the table in front of her.

She waved the guards off and they withdrew.

After silently staring at him for a full minute, she said, "You're the first, and so far only, thief to take my bait. I'm uncertain whether that makes you brave or stupid. Perhaps a little of both."

"So you had Tobias send me here?" Gareth asked.

"I have no idea who that is. No, I had a 'wayward' servant spread the news of my newest acquisition through the rougher parts of the city on the assumption that someone like you would make an appearence. We've been waiting for over a week and as I said you're the only one to show up."

If his legs were longer, Gareth would have happily kicked himself. "Okay, you caught me. What do you need a thief for? You're the richest woman in the city. I can't imagine there's anything you can't just buy."

"In the city, you're quite correct. But what I want isn't in the city." He stayed silent, waiting for her to go on. "Are you familiar with Amet Sur?"

He debated lying then shook his head. "Who is he, some foreign merchant?"

"Hardly. Amet Sur was the first Arcane Lord, a contemporary of Lord Colt."

Gareth knew Colt's name of course. The whole bloody continent was named after the man. "Okay, so what's a long-dead wizard got to do with me?"

"I'm mounting an expedition to plunder one of his palaces. I need a thief to deal with any traps. You made it into my museum without getting hit by a poison dart. That argues for at least a minimal level of skill."

"I suppose bowing out gracefully isn't an option?"

"It is. If you decline my offer of employment, I won't force you. I will, however, have you hung for the thief you are. What will it be?"

As if he had a choice. Maybe he'd find an opportunity to escape later. "I'd be delighted to join your expedition. When do we leave?"

"Soon. There's one more person I need to hire before you depart."

Gareth grinned despite his situation. "Will you be hiring them the same way you did me?"

"No." The chill in her voice froze him to the core. "Approaching her will take a good deal more tact. Happily, I believe I have just the prize to tempt her. But first…"

Melisandre reached down and placed a bracelet of shiny metal on the table.

"What's this?" Gareth asked.

"A control bracelet. As long as you have it on, my wizards can find you anywhere you might try to flee. Consider it an insurance policy. Put it on."

"You don't trust me?"

"Put it on."

She wasn't making a request and his options hadn't gotten any better. He picked up the bracelet, enjoying the cool feel of the metal. On the inside of the band, someone had carved fine markings he didn't recognize.

At last he slid it over his hand. The band shrunk all by itself until the fit was snug, but not uncomfortable.

"Good." She slid his dagger and other gear back to him. "Now we need to go talk to the sea witch."

The blood drained from Gareth's face. Maybe he should have taken his chances with the noose.

———

There was an area down by the docks where no one went, mostly because the people that did go there seldom came back. Every street kid knew the legend of the sea witch. She was supposed to be a hag more dead than alive, her servants shambling in mockery of the living. Not having a death wish, Gareth never made the trip to see for himself. A couple of his friends had claimed to have caught a glimpse of one of her zombies, but he doubted it.

Had he planned to pay the legendary witch a visit, he wouldn't have chosen to come calling after midnight. But his new employer insisted that they were more likely to find the witch up and in a good mood after the sunset. Hopefully she was right, but from the looks of fear twisting the faces of the guards she brought along, they didn't seem optimistic. Even worse, Melisandre had only brought four of them. Had it been up to Gareth, they would have brought a small army.

But nothing was up to him anymore. The moment he put the bracelet on, he lost his freedom. That he got to keep breathing, in hindsight, seemed insufficient compensation. Maybe when they found this treasure they were supposed to be looking for, he could help himself to a little bonus.

A block away from the forbidden section of the boardwalk,

a thick, wet fog rose slowly from the ground. It came out of nowhere, like magic. Since they were going to visit a witch, he shouldn't have been surprised.

They hadn't seen a soul out and about for the last fifteen minutes. Maybe it was because of the hour and maybe it was because the locals had more sense than them, but either way Gareth envied those behind closed, hopefully heavily barred doors.

To try and break some of the tension, Gareth turned to Melisandre and asked, "So was the statue of silver or mithril?"

"There never was a statue, I just allowed that rumor to spread. Now be quiet, we're getting close."

Shapes appeared, moving through the fog like ghosts. They seemed unsteady, moving jerkily like puppets handled by a beginning puppeteer. The first one stepped out of the fog and into the light. Its skin sagged and where its eyes should have been, there were only gaping holes filled with glowing red light. It wore tattered clothes that might once have been a sailor's uniform. Somehow the creature didn't stink. That seemed impossible, but he wouldn't complain.

The guards drew their swords and formed a circle around Melisandre. "We should retreat, Mistress."

"Idiot. These are the witch's minions. We have to be getting close to her home. As long as they make no aggressive moves towards us, you will make none towards them. Understood?"

The guards nodded but made no effort to sheathe their swords. How much good they'd do against already dead opponents, Gareth didn't know, but he doubted it would be much.

If it came to a fight, he figured they were already dead.

A path opened in the fog, inviting them deeper into the witch's domain. Not an invitation any sane person would be eager to accept, but Melisandre strode forward without a hint of fear. She was either the bravest person Gareth had ever met, or she simply couldn't imagine anyone daring to harm her. Most likely it was the latter. He'd met a few powerful people, and to a person they all imagined they were invincible.

The problem with that attitude was that you only had to be wrong once.

Something squeaked under his feet. Gareth looked down and sure enough they'd reached the boardwalk. This section appeared as rotten as the zombie he'd caught a glimpse of. Hopefully he didn't put a foot wrong and end up in the drink.

At last a light blossomed in front of them. The fog parted, revealing a woman seated on a crude stool beside a green fire that turned Gareth's stomach when he looked at it. He nearly whistled when they moved closer. If this was the sea witch, he'd been badly deceived. She looked around thirty, with pale, smooth skin, a pretty face, a fine figure mostly hidden by a simple black dress, and eyes that glowed the same green as the fire.

"You have great nerve coming to my home uninvited, Melisandre Raven," the sea witch said. "Tell me why I shouldn't simply add you and your companions to my collection."

"I'm here to trade," Melisandre said. "Will you not at least hear me out?"

Though her voice stayed steady and cool, Melisandre's left hand clenched and relaxed over and over. For his part, so powerful was the witch's presence, it took all Gareth's willpower not to piss himself.

"My time is valuable," the witch said. "Have you brought something to pay for it?"

Melisandre gestured at the guards. "You can have these four."

"Mis—"

The guard's exclamation was cut off by arms that seemed to come from nowhere. They wrapped around the mercenaries' heads and arms, dragging them out of sight before they could even react.

Sounds of struggle filled the fog followed by splashes, then silence.

Gareth swallowed. While he'd harbored no illusions about the loyalty of his new employer, that was cold-blooded beyond anything he'd imagined.

"Very well," the witch said when silence had once again descended. "Make your offer."

"You are familiar with Amet Sur?" Melisandre asked.

"Every wizard worthy of the name knows of the first and greatest Arcane Lord."

"I am preparing an expedition to his capital. I have my trap-removal expert. Now I need a wizard. Since you are the most powerful in the city, naturally I came to you. What do you say?"

"I have no desire to leave my home and travel halfway around the world to some dusty desert, only to collect some gold trinkets to line your pockets."

"Not even for the Sanguine Scroll?" Melisandre asked.

The witch stood, her green eyes flashing. "Don't speak of it even in jest. Any wizard would give their right arm for that scroll."

"I assure you my offer is serious. According to my agents in the City of Coins, Eddred of Markane has a map provided by Lord Valtan and orders to retrieve the Scroll. With your help, we could kill Eddred and seize any treasure along with the Scroll for ourselves. I'm no wizard so the Scroll has little value for me. Help me, and it's yours."

"The Sanguine Scroll." The witch muttered more to herself

than them. She looked intrigued. Hopefully that meant Gareth would make it out of this creepy place in one piece.

"Agreed," the witch said at last.

"Excellent. I've arranged a high-speed caravan to transport the two of you across the country to a minor port of no particular interest where one of my ships is waiting to carry you across the ocean. The journey should take a month at most. When you arrive, you'll meet with the final member of your team along with my mercenaries."

"And where will you be during all this?" the witch asked.

"Here, eagerly awaiting news of your success."

Great. Him and the witch together for heaven only knew how long. Maybe Gareth could convince her to remove his bracelet. Then again, considering her price for a simple conversation, maybe he'd learn to live with it.

CHAPTER 3

L ady White strode across the sands of the Dead Lands. Nothingness surrounded her in every direction. In all her many years she had never been in a place so totally devoid of life. Even back home, the twisted, demonic denizens of the city radiated a sort of life. But not here. Here there was sand, ghouls, and not much else.

She looked up at the clear, blue sky. At least the weather was nice. Somehow she felt it should be cloudy or maybe an eternal night sky. Instead it looked normal, aside from the lack of birds. She didn't know what she thought she'd find when she agreed to allow Otto to drop her off here, but this wasn't it.

Her warbeast butted her with its head and she stroked it. "At least I have you for company."

Though one of its legs was still missing, her beast had regained most of its strength. The richness of the corruption tainting the ether allowed it to heal quickly.

Speaking of corruption, something shifted up ahead. Not in the sand, but in the ether. She peered harder. No ghouls this time. Whatever approached was stronger, more subtle as well.

Perhaps her chance had finally come to find a source of information capable of setting her on the correct path. Weeks of roaming the wastelands was getting old.

Darkness gathered ten paces ahead of her, took on the shape of a man, and became solid. He... it... whatever this creature was, it felt like it was made of pure corruption. A demon then? It wouldn't surprise her to find a few wandering this wretched place.

"Name yourself, pawn of Astaroth," the black figure said. "The guardian of this land commands you."

Power gathered around Lady White. "No one commands me, save Astaroth himself."

They lashed out at the same moment.

Streams of corruption collided at the midpoint between them.

She grimaced and took a step back. No demon or undead had forced her back in many years. Whatever she faced, it had tremendous power.

Powerful or not, she refused to be beaten by a shade. "Astaroth, help me."

Her patron answered. A portal opened inside of her, flooding Lady White with corruption. It felt like Astaroth put his hands on her shoulders. With her master helping, any loss would be an insult to him. And that was something Lady White refused to allow.

She took a step forward, shaping her magic into a wedge and parting the creature's strike.

Like a sword, her spell sliced through the enemy's magic until its form appeared before her.

It tried to raise a shield, but too slowly.

She stabbed into the core of its being and clenched her fist, crushing its essence.

Though it made no sound, the monster's pain flooded into her, giving her strength.

"Submit!" she commanded.

It fought harder, trying to scour the life from her. But Lady White had no life in her and she kept squeezing until the flow of corruption from her foe vanished.

"I yield," it said at last.

She didn't lower her guard in the slightest. "Where is Amet Sur's capital?"

"Another grave robber." The spirit sounded dejected. "I had hoped for more from someone capable of besting me."

Astaroth's power wavered. She had little time. "Answer the question." She squeezed its essence again to emphasize her order.

"You're nearly there. Just keep going due north from here. Another week at most will see you there."

"Are there more guardians?" She silently begged Astaroth not to abandon her yet.

"Many more, though none as powerful as me."

She nodded, hardly surprised. "I'm going to release you now. Leave, and never show yourself again. Should we encounter each other a second time, I will not be so merciful."

"How considerate." When she released her grip on its essence, the creature sank slowly into the sand.

When it had fully gone, she dropped to her knees and leaned against her warbeast. Astaroth's presence had vanished along with the creature, leaving her feeling hollowed out and weak. After such an intervention, she wouldn't be able to call on her master directly for some time.

Should she encounter another guardian even half as strong as the first, she might be in trouble.

Her warbeast growled and crouched, facing the spot where

the creature had vanished. She'd been so diminished by the battle that she hadn't even sensed the gathering power. Now that she focused on it, she knew exactly what it was. The guardian hadn't fled, it had hidden, waiting for her moment of weakness.

The sand rose, taking on the shape of a dragon. Black flames flickered where its eyes should have been.

Lady White had neither time nor strength to react before it crashed down, swallowing her whole.

———

W hen Lady White came to, she was surprised to find herself in some sort of cavern rather than in hell awaiting Astaroth's judgement. She didn't hurt anywhere, so whatever attacked her must have used purely physical means. Only magic could hurt her undead body.

She looked around, the total darkness no impediment to her undead eyes. The cavern wasn't especially large, maybe thirty feet in diameter. The walls appeared covered in claw marks, as if some titanic beast gouged the chamber out of solid stone. The air carried a hint of rot. She was clearly not alone down here, but where were the other undead? They might be anywhere in these tunnels. Lucky for her, most undead had no interest in others of their kind. Generally, they preferred to hunt the living

Lady White focused on the link between her and her warbeast. The connection remained strong, but she guessed they were now separated by miles. Where had the guardian spirit brought her? Hopefully not several miles straight down.

Speaking of the guardian, she couldn't sense its presence. Maybe Lady White would be lucky and it destroyed itself in the process of sending her here. Her smile was bitter. Lately her luck had only gone in one direction, bad.

At least there was an exit. A single tunnel just wide enough for her to pass through led out of the cavern. With no other options, she set out. Her shoulders nearly brushed the tunnel walls. Lucky for her she wasn't the claustrophobic sort. It helped that she had no need to breathe.

As she walked through the dark, silent passage, she considered her next move. Her options didn't fill her with hope. There had to be something dangerous in the tunnels. The only reason for the guardian to drag her here was to let something else kill her.

Hour after hour of slogging had her wondering if instead her enemy expected her to die of boredom. Miles of undifferentiated tunnel seemed to extend forever. She didn't have to worry about getting lost at least. There hadn't been a branch or fork yet. On the plus side, every hour that passed let her power recover that much more.

She risked using a little of that power to peer into the ether. The corruption here was every bit as thick as everywhere else in the Dead Lands. There was no sign of the guardian spirit. If it was as worn out as her, it would take a long time to recover.

Wishful thinking perhaps.

At last, after so many hours she'd stopped bothering to try and keep track, the tunnel opened into another cavern, this one vaster by several orders of magnitude. She found herself on a ledge looking down into it. She had no way to continue on, at least not on this level. Even worse, the chamber wasn't empty.

Hundreds of ghouls filled it, snarling and clambering over each other. They reminded her more of insects than former men. Lady White had never seen this many ghouls in one place. They usually hunted and traveled in packs of eight to fifteen. Sometime more and sometimes less, but never in the hundreds. If she could command them, she would have an unstoppable army.

She started to reach out with her magic only to catch herself. Even at her strongest she'd never commanded undead on this scale. Weakened as she was, all she'd manage was to get herself torn apart.

Setting aside ambition for survival, she focused on the solitary exit from the chamber, another narrow tunnel on the far side of the ghoul horde.

Subtlety would be called for here. Wrapping herself in corruption, she hopped off the ledge and glided down toward the tunnel entrance.

The ghouls never looked up as she floated over their heads.

It wasn't until she reached the halfway point that her magic started to give out. Cursing her weakness and the guardian that had drained her, she picked a spot free of scrabbling ghouls and landed.

Hidden by a shield of corruption, she eased forward.

Gentle touches guided the ghouls out of her way.

One particularly large specimen stopped directly in front of her and sniffed.

Lady White froze.

She didn't dare try and nudge it aside.

Instead she reached out to a small ghoul and drove a blade of pure corruption into its half-rotten brain.

The undead went mad.

It charged the larger ghoul, slamming into it and trying to claw it to pieces.

The two of them ended up in a heap of snarling flesh.

Lady White seized the moment, slipping around them and making a final dash for the tunnel.

Only when she was a safe distance away from the ghoul pit did she relax a fraction.

That was one challenge down and no doubt many more to go.

CHAPTER 4

T he heat baking the City of Coins hadn't lessened
during King Eddred of Markane's nearly yearlong
absence. He still started sweating the moment he
took a step. The people seemed completely unaware that he
had been at least indirectly the cause of their troubles last year.
He still felt terrible that his quest for revenge had led to so
many deaths. At least his visit this time wouldn't lead to a near
invasion.

Today found him once again in the warehouse he'd rented
to serve as his base of operations. It would serve as such until
he advanced into the desert. Assuming that ever happened. His
confidence in his mission was waning by the day.

The warehouse held weapons, supplies, and everything else
they'd need to begin the mission. Now all he needed were
soldiers. He'd interviewed half the mercenary captains in the
city and to a person, the moment he mentioned going beyond
the city walls, they walked out.

He stared as the most recent mercenary he'd interviewed
stomped off. They'd been here for nearly a month trying to

secure sufficient forces to recover the Sanguine Scroll from Amet Sur's capital. He had a map and magic to keep the undead at bay and still no one would take the job. Maybe he should have hired mercenaries elsewhere and brought them here.

Not that there was an excess of mercenaries available. If he so much as showed his face in the New Garen Empire—Eddred nearly gagged when he thought of the continent in those terms—he'd be arrested and quickly hung. No, he had to find what he needed here. That was unfortunately easier said than done.

"Majesty?" Adam, one of his two wizard bodyguards asked. "Shall we call it a day?"

Eddred stretched until his back popped. "Are there any more captains waiting?"

"Let me check." Adam closed his eyes and a moment later said, "There's one more just approaching. Should I tell him to come back tomorrow?"

"Heaven's mercy, no. We're not doing so well that we can afford to offend a potential ally. By all means invite him in. Where is Uther anyway?"

"With the whores." Adam stared up at the ceiling as if praying for strength. "I believe his exact words were, 'No one's stupid enough to take this job anyway, so why do I need to evaluate them?'"

Eddred understood Adam's feelings. Uther had gotten less and less enthusiastic as the weeks dragged by. He wanted to kill Otto Shenk, not hire mercenaries and go wandering around in the desert to potentially get eaten by ghouls. Not that Eddred figured that was likely since they had Lord Valtan's magic to protect them.

"That's fine. I'm sure I can manage on my own. I've had

plenty of practice since we arrived. Invite the new arrival in, won't you, Adam?"

The wizard bowed and walked over to the warehouse door. He returned a minute later with a tall, pale, bald man. Hilts of daggers jutted up out of the mercenary's boots, a sword was strapped to his back, and a hatchet hung from a loop on his belt. His armor was simple hardened leather. Anything heavier would roast him alive in the southern heat. As it was, the stink of sweat wafting off the man curled Eddred's nose hairs.

Eddred stood and held out a hand. "Welcome, sir. And thank you for answering my call."

The mercenary's hand engulfed Eddred's when they shook. He got the distinct impression that if the mercenary had wanted to, he could have crushed every bone in Eddred's hand with little effort.

"Majesty," the man said. "I'm Captain Kane of The Black Sword Company. Is it true you're planning an expedition into the desert?"

"It is. Which explains my distinct lack of success in hiring soldiers. I'd all but given up until you arrived. If you knew the mission, why did you come?"

"We're not from the city," Kane said. "Myself and my men are all northerners. I know Lord Valtan's reputation. If you have something magical that he says will keep the monsters at bay, I'm willing to trust he knows what he's about."

A huge weight lifted off Eddred's shoulders. He gestured to the empty chair. "Please, have a seat and we can discuss the details."

"Thank you." Kane sat, shifting slightly so the hatchet didn't poke him in the side. "When are you looking to set out?"

"As soon as possible. In truth, I had hoped to be underway by now."

"I see." Kane scratched his scruffy beard. "You may not want to hire me then. Most of my men are off on another job. They should be back in a month, six weeks at the most. I had hoped to have another job lined up for when they got back. But if you're in a hurry, I understand if you want to look elsewhere."

"I will keep looking," Eddred said. "But given that you're the only person to even consider taking on the mission, I hold out little hope. Can I offer you a small retainer to ensure you're still available if I haven't departed when your soldiers arrive? How many men do you have under arms?"

"Fifty. Forty of them are currently out to sea protecting a fleet of three merchant ships," Kane said. "'I'll take ten pounds of gold, nonrefundable. That's twenty-five percent of our fee."

"Five," Eddred countered.

"Seven, and not an ounce less."

"Agreed. Adam, fetch Captain Kane's gold." Eddred didn't regret the potential loss of gold, he had plenty to spare after all. The loss of a possible six weeks was another matter altogether. Heaven only knew what Otto Shenk was getting up to.

Whatever it was, it couldn't be good.

———

L ate in the afternoon, after finishing his business at the whorehouse and swinging by the warehouse only to find it empty, Uther headed for the ship. The scent of the ocean and rotting fish filled the air as he neared the docks. Whether it was the heat or dryness of the air, the city docks stank less than some ports Uther had visited. In fact, it smelled marginally better than the whorehouse. Though the dock workers left a great deal to be desired in the looks department.

Even though they'd been in the City of Coins for almost

two months—months during which they'd accomplished almost nothing—Eddred still insisted on sleeping on the ship. Uther didn't know why and he didn't especially care. He could sleep there as well as anywhere else.

Despite how different the city was from Straken, or maybe because of how different it was, Uther found he quite liked his temporary home. The women were beautiful and the people generally friendly even as they tried to gain every advantage during negotiations. He wouldn't mind calling this place home.

Only the knowledge that his father still rotted in a mine back in Straken, assuming the old king still lived, held him back. Otto Shenk had to pay for that. How he was going to make the miserable bastard suffer was another matter. Wizards were simply beyond his skills.

"Good of you to join us." Adam, Eddred's wizard body-guard, stood at the ship's rail, his white robe plastered to his back.

"Did I miss anything interesting?"

"We found a potential mercenary company. They're currently out of the city, but their captain has expressed interest in our mission when they return. Eddred has paid a retainer to ensure they don't take another job."

"He paid them before I could evaluate? That wasn't the deal."

Adam shrugged. "You were otherwise occupied. We haven't had so many people leaping at our offer that His Majesty wanted to risk letting this group get away."

Uther winced at the subtle critique. He couldn't deny a certain lack of interest lately. The whole mission, running Valtan's errands, all of it seemed pointless. The passage of weeks without results did little to improve his feelings. That needed to change. On his own, Eddred was liable to lead them all to failure.

"Do you remember the company's name? I'll do a little digging tonight."

"They're called The Black Sword and their captain's name is Kane. All northerners from the sounds of it."

"A band of mercenaries from our neck of the woods? Shouldn't be hard to find out about them. We tend to stand out in this part of the world."

"Best of luck." Adam pushed away from the rail and walked out of sight.

The wizard's disdain annoyed Uther, but he couldn't deny some of it was well deserved. He resolved to focus on his job and to that end turned away from the ship and headed back to the city. When in doubt, a tavern was often the best place to find information. Though in this city, it would probably cost more than a mug of ale.

The shadows were long when Uther reached his chosen watering hole. A sign featuring a mug dangling from a sword's quillon hung over the door.

He'd noticed it in passing a few times as he made his way to his favorite whorehouse. The men he'd seen hanging around outside looked rough and ready for a fight. Maybe not mercenaries, but the sort of people that would know where to find them.

The thugs glared at Uther as he pushed through the bead door and into the common room. There was a fair crowd considering the early hour. A dozen men of the same sort as those outside sat in groups of three or four around the room. The only women were the servers and they'd all seen better days. Of course, he might just be biased given the company he'd been keeping lately.

Behind the bar, a tall, tan man with a thick beard and broad chest stood keeping watch on the patrons. He looked more like a bouncer than a barkeep. In fact, if Uther didn't know better, he would have sworn the man was of Straken ancestry.

Smiling, he ambled up to the bar and slapped down a silver coin. "Mead if you have it."

The bartender took the coin and put it on a scale. "You want change or credit?"

"I want information."

"You'd best have gold to go with your silver, foreigner."

"If you have the information I need, rest assured, I can pay. Speaking of foreigners, you don't look local yourself." Uther held out his hand. "Uther of Straken."

"You have a good eye." The bartender shook but didn't offer his name. "My grandfather moved here from Straken."

"Interesting. Our people seldom travel far from home. Do you know why he left?"

"That the information you want to buy?"

"Hardly. I was just trying to make conversation. What I want is any information you have about The Black Sword mercenary company. Where I can find their headquarters would be a good start."

"That all? One ounce of gold will cover it."

Uther placed a gold coin on the bar but slapped his hand over it when the bartender tried to take it. "After I hear what I'm buying."

The big man shrugged. "Kane set up shop here about ten years ago. Hired down-on-their-luck foreigners. He got a reputation as a man that did the job without asking too many questions."

"Mercenaries have a reputation for keeping their mouths shut. What makes Kane so special?"

"He'll take any job, no matter how dangerous. Especially since he never goes into the field. He just arranges the men. If they don't all come back, more gold for him."

"That's pretty cold-blooded. What do the men working for him think?" Uther asked.

"There are always more desperate men. The locals don't like hiring foreigners. They don't trust them. That means Kane is the only game in town."

The more Uther heard the less he liked it. "Where can I find their base?"

"A warehouse down by the docks. It's in the northwest district. Pretty rough and run down. There's a big sword of blackened iron hanging over the entrance. Can't miss it."

"Thanks." Uther lifted his hand off the coin and the bartender took it.

"A pleasure to be of service, my prince." The bartender grinned at Uther's reaction. "What, did you think no one knew who you were? The whole city's talking about you and Eddred of Markane and your crazy quest. You came a long way just to die in the desert."

"I have no intention of dying in the desert." Uther turned and stalked out.

Once he was outside, he took a deep breath of the slightly cooler night air. Now that he knew a little about Kane, he wanted to talk to the man as soon as possible. If only so he could tell Eddred to find someone else.

The walk across the city took Uther most of half an hour. For the past ten minutes, the neighborhood had grown steadily worse. The sour stench of vomit and piss nearly overwhelmed the pungent scent of the sea. It seemed even the richest cities had their slums.

He hadn't seen any guards in a while, but that didn't overly concern him. Uther had his sword and knew how to use it. He might be a little rusty, it was true, but if there was a thug skilled enough to take him down, then he deserved to bleed out in a ditch.

So far all he'd gotten for his trouble was the occasional sullen glare thrown from darkened alleys. The predators must have recognized the threat he represented. They wanted easy marks, not a fight.

At last, he reached the warehouse the bartender described. The black iron sword wasn't a sword at all. Rather someone had welded two pieces of pig iron into the general shape of a sword and hung it on the wall. It seemed Captain Kane cut corners wherever possible. Given what little he knew, Uther expected no better.

The warehouse itself appeared to be in good shape. At least it didn't appear in danger of falling down at the first sign of wind. The wood was blackened by a thick coat of tar. That no doubt served to protect it from the salt breeze blowing in from the harbor. Of course, should a fireball hit it, the place would go up like a torch.

A pair of double doors twice as tall as Uther served as the main entrance. Off to one side, a smaller door allowed for people to come and go without having to drag the big ones open. He walked over and knocked.

Someone must have been on duty as only seconds passed before a small slot in the door slid open. A pair of narrow, bloodshot eyes glared out. "What do you want?"

"I'd like to speak with Captain Kane. He met with my business partner this morning and I need to go over the details of the job."

The doorman muttered something under his breath then asked, "Name?"

"I'm Uther. The man he met with is Eddred. He already received a down payment so a little conversation shouldn't be an issue."

"Oh, yeah, the lunatics heading out into the desert. Man, I'm glad I only work the door." The slot slammed shut and the door opened. "Come on. The captain's in back in his office."

Uther followed the pudgy doorman towards the rear of the warehouse. Racks of swords, bows, and armor lined one side of the warehouse while rows of bunk beds lined the other. It looked like The Black Sword had fully converted the warehouse into a proper barracks. He couldn't deny being impressed. Given what he'd been told by the bartender, Uther had expected the mercenaries' base to be a complete mess. At the very least, they appeared well equipped and competent.

The pair stopped in front of a closed door. The doorman knocked and when it opened, a grizzly looking bearded fellow glared out. "Can I help you?"

His voice sounded completely at odds with his appearance. He reminded Uther of some of Father's courtiers. "I'm Eddred's partner. I hoped to discuss some of the details of the mission with you."

Kane brightened. "So you've decided to give us the job? Splendid! Come in, come in."

The mercenary captain waved off his door guard and ushered Uther into his office. The space measured maybe ten yards square. A fine table carved with knights and dragons dominated the room. The massive table wouldn't have looked out of place in the home of a noble. Comfortable leather chairs and a cabinet filled with books and ledgers completed the decorations.

Kane guided Uther into a chair in the corner then sat across from him. "I gathered from what His Majesty said that you would still be exploring your options. Why did you decide to go with us?"

"I never said we did." At Kane's scowl Uther continued. "I was busy when Uther interviewed you and I wanted to discuss a few details that came to my attention. Specifically, your rather poor reputation regarding your men's survival."

"Whatever negative things you may have heard, I promise you it wasn't from any of my previous clients. We have always done exactly what we promised. As to the survival of my men, mercenary work is dangerous. Naturally not everyone makes it through every battle."

"And you avoiding the field? I can't imagine that gets you much loyalty."

Kane scrubbed a hand across his face.

"Look. All this." He waved at himself. "It's a part. Clients expect a mercenary captain to have a certain appearance. I'm just giving them what they want. I've never swung a sword in battle. Hell, I've rarely swung one in practice. I'm a businessman and this is a costume. I assure you, my unit commanders are far better at war than I am. And my clients are all better off without me in the field."

Uther certainly believed that last sentence. As for the rest of it, he couldn't deny that it made sense. While he considered Kane a lowlife and opportunist, he also felt confident that he'd deliver what he promised.

He stood and held out his hand. "Thank you, Captain. Your setup might be unorthodox, but I feel much better about our potential business. Assuming that no one else shows up in the meantime, I'm going to recommend Eddred accept your offer."

Kane gave his hand an enthusiastic pump. "Thank you. I'm pleased to have earned your trust. Rest assured, you won't regret hiring The Black Sword."

Uther seriously hoped not. If anything went wrong with Valtan's magic, those mercenaries would be the only thing between him and heaven only knew how many ghouls.

CHAPTER 5

Gareth could easily learn to hate the ocean. He stood in the front of their transport and let the salty spray hit him in the face. This was what passed for entertainment on board. He would have promised to devote himself to charitable works if it would have summoned a whore, some good brandy, and a trio of card players. Unfortunately, he didn't know which of the archangels to pray to for that miracle.

After traveling across Colt's Land in a wagon pulled day and night by enchanted metal horses, he and the sea witch had arrived at a little port city exactly halfway between two of the city-states. It looked like the sort of place where no questions were asked. He'd visited enough taverns with that reputation to recognize the feel. No one would meet your eye and if you looked too long the flash of bared steel would soon move your gaze along.

The moment they arrived, they were taken to the docks where a silver ship equipped with oars operated by mechanical rowers waited. It had no sails and a crew of only five. No one spoke to them when they boarded. The ship launched at once and traveled at rapid speed across the water.

In his many hours alone, he tried cutting through the mithril band that served as Melisandre's shackle. His black-bladed dagger, usually more than capable of slicing through whatever needed cutting, including steel, couldn't even scratch the bracelet. That was just one of many disappointments he'd faced since departing.

Now, a month after they set out, the walls of the City of Coins appeared in the distance. And thank goodness for that. One more day with nothing to do and no one to talk to might have driven him crazy. Or maybe crazier. You'd have thought the sea witch might have liked to chat since they were the only ones on board who knew the true purpose of their mission. But you'd have been wrong.

Speaking of his taciturn traveling companion, the green-eyed bitch strode out from belowdecks and looked around at the empty deck. He didn't know what she expected to find. The crew kept to the control room or looked after the enchanted rowers one level down.

Maybe one last attempt at conversation would be worth-while. They would be relying on each other in the field.

He ambled down on deck, wearing his best smile. She was wearing a black dress that covered her from neck to ankle. How did she stand it in this miserable heat? He'd never felt anything like it, even in the depths of summer back home. She also had a lovely figure and it seemed a shame not to show it off a little.

Gareth gave a shudder. He really had been on board for too long.

"Looks like we're almost there," he said.

She glanced at him, her eyes flared a fraction brighter, and she looked away.

Right.

"Look, we're going to be out there on our own. Can't you at least tell me your name? I mean, if I need to shout a warning, 'Look out, Sea Witch,' seems a bit clunky."

At last, she focused on him. He controlled an overwhelming desire to flee only by the narrowest of margins. Maybe he shouldn't have pestered her.

"You make a lot of noise," she said. "I thought thieves were supposed to be quiet."

"Oh, I'm very quiet when I'm working. There isn't really anyone to sneak up on here. We haven't been properly introduced. I'm Gareth."

She ignored his proffered hand. "If I tell you my name, will you be quiet?"

"As a mouse."

"You may call me Ginevera."

He brightened and fell silent. It wasn't much, but it was a start.

———

Four hours later, after a brief interview with a nervous harbor patrol captain, the ship tied up at the City of Coins dock. Gareth hardly had patience enough to wait for the crew to finish tying them up before he hurried down the gangplank. Solid ground at last. What a relief.

The sea witch, or rather Ginevera, joined him at a more sedate pace. She looked around, taking everything in and seeming to dismiss it. Being a super-strong wizard probably meant you couldn't let on how impressive you found a mere city.

Gareth had no such restrictions and he gaped at the walls, the buildings, the people, everything. It was all so different from back home. Everything was made out of tan stone and dark wood. The people dressed in bright clothes as if determined to make up for the lack of color in their buildings. And the heat, heaven help him. Gareth feared he might melt before they reached wherever they were going. At least the smell of the docks was familiar, if muted compared to back home. Rotting fish was clearly a universal feature of port cities the world over.

The ship's captain, he'd never bothered introducing himself, came down the ramp to join them. He wore a crisp gray tunic and white trousers. Somehow, despite the heat, he looked as fresh as a daisy. Bastard!

"If you'll follow me," he said. "I can take you to Ms. Raven's warehouse."

Gareth and Ginevera fell in behind him and started down the docks. They passed other tied-up vessels, all traditional sailing ships, drawing looks from bare-chested stevedores, and generally making far too big an impression for Gareth's liking.

"You're going to be here when we get back, right?" Gareth asked.

"My orders are to wait four months," the captain said. "If you haven't returned by then, I'm to carry word of your failure back to Ms. Raven."

"I do not fail," the sea witch said.

Gareth shivered despite the heat, so chilled was her voice.

The Raven Company warehouse sat right on the water to allow for easy loading and unloading. Heavy block and tackle hung from a beam nearly two feet thick jutting over the water.

They seemed to have arrived during a lull as there wasn't a ship in sight. That being the case, why hadn't they just come directly here?

He shrugged as the captain led them to a side door and knocked. He exchanged a few words with someone inside then turned to Gareth and Ginevera. "The third member of your group has already arrived. Ms. Raven's agent in the city will be joining you within the hour for a full briefing. If you'll excuse me."

The captain hurried back toward his ship as if eager to be done with his passengers. Gareth couldn't really blame the man. Ginevera wasn't exactly the sort of passenger he would have preferred to travel with either. Unfortunately they were stuck with each other.

The warehouse door opened wider, giving him a better look at the man inside. He was tall, broad shouldered, and dressed in canvas shorts with his hairless chest bare. In fact, the only hair on the fellow was a little patch directly under his lower lip.

"Come in, come in." He waved them through the open door. "Our other guest arrived two days ago. He doesn't seem the patient sort, so the sooner I can get you lot on your way, the better for everyone."

Finally, someone sensibly terrified. Gareth had begun to think he was the only one with brains enough to realize how much trouble they were in. He hurried through the door and Ginevera strolled along behind him. Inside, the warehouse looked like any other Gareth had robbed over the years. Light shone down through skylights, illuminating crates stacked everywhere in neat piles.

The warehouse manager hustled ahead of them toward the rear of the warehouse. "This way."

"I'm Gar—"

"Don't tell me!" he said. "I don't want to know your names. I don't want you to know my name. Ms. Raven made it clear I was to provide whatever help you needed and I will, but the less I know about this madness the better. She's already insanely rich. Why in the world does she need to do something crazy like this?"

He shook his bald head and kept walking without looking back. The way he talked, you'd think they were dragging him out into the desert with them.

At the rear of the warehouse, in a deep, dark corner, a table sat in the shadows. Seated at it was a vaguely human-shaped shadow.

"The rest of your party is here, sir, I'll leave you to get aquatinted. As soon as your contact shows up I'll bring him back."

With that explosion of anxious words, the manager hurried back the way he'd come.

Ginevera brushed past Gareth and stared down at the shadow. "You're strong. I can see the corruption swirling around you. Which demon lord do you serve?"

The shadow man looked up, revealing a pale face so handsome Gareth's heart skipped a beat. He couldn't be human.

"I serve Astaroth," the man said in a voice as perfect as his face. "Lord of the Dead commanded me to come here and join with your group. Your master's spies will find the renegade and I will destroy her. Nothing else matters. As long as you do nothing to interfere, you will survive this mission. Get in my way and I won't hesitate to kill you both."

Lightning crackled around the sea witch's hands. "One, I have no master. Two, I don't take threats lightly. If you imagine I'll be easy to kill, think again."

The man stood and Gareth finally realized that the reason he looked like a living shadow was the loose, flowing cloak he wore. It covered everything from his neck down to his black boots. Darkness swirled around his hands. Just looking at it made Gareth nauseous.

"Hey, guys, we're all on the same team here, right?" Gareth asked. "Maybe you could wait until after we finish the job to kill each other."

Glowing eyes, one pair green and the other red, turned to glare at Gareth.

He winced. Should've kept his mouth shut.

"Your human has a point." The shadow man sat back down and some of the tension drained away. "Any power I wasted on killing you would only increase the chances of failing my mission and that must not happen. You may call me Jackal. If you wish to continue this after my prey is slain, I will be happy to oblige."

For a moment he feared the sea witch wanted to continue it right now, but slowly the lightning vanished and she sat opposite Jackal. "Ginevera. And as long as you don't insult me again, I will let your offense go this once."

Gareth let out a breath. "Great. I'm Gareth, by the way. Nice to meet you. I'm sure you've got some great stories to tell. Should make the trip more interesting."

Jackal turned his burning gaze on Gareth who found he suddenly couldn't breathe. "I am not a bard to sing for your amusement. Now sit and be silent."

Ginevera's lip quirked up a fraction.

At least the two of them agreed on one thing. Pity it seemed to be hating him.

51

Before the silence around the table grew too uncomfortable, the door opened behind them. Gareth looked over his shoulder but made out little beyond the nearly blinding glow of the sun. A silhouette appeared in the doorway then it closed again.

Footsteps filled the silent warehouse and a figure passed through the shafts of light from the skylights. Gareth got the impression of armor and weapons but little else. This must be their employer's agent. With any luck he'd tell them what they all wanted to hear: that they could set out at once.

He stopped a few feet from the table. No one stood and as usual no introductions were made. Gareth really didn't understand that last part. After all, it was nice to have a name to go with a face. Certainly it was better than pointing and saying "hey you."

"Gentlemen and lady," the man said. "Our mutual benefactor has entrusted me with acquiring the information you need to find Amet Sur's capital. You'll be happy to know I've secured access to Eddred of Markane's mission. In fact, my mercenaries will be making up the bulk of his party. Signs will be left for you to follow."

The guy looked like a thug but spoke like a banker. The weirdness of it made Gareth's head hurt.

"How soon can we leave?" Jackal asked.

"Three days?" the agent said. "Eddred's party will leave tomorrow and you'll want to let them get a little ways ahead so they don't notice you following along. A confrontation before you reach the city wouldn't do, after all."

Jackal growled but offered no complaint. The sea witch didn't speak at all.

Curious, Gareth asked, "Why are you betraying your employer?"

"Betray? Bite your tongue. My contract specifically states that the mercenaries I provide are there to fight undead and act as bearers. Nowhere does it state that I have to keep the mission a secret."

"I doubt your employer will see it that way," Gareth said.

The man shrugged. "If Eddred was worried about this sort of thing, he should have included it in the contract. If you all will excuse me, I have arrangements to make. When the time is right, I'll return to set you on the correct path."

He bowed and hurried back the way he'd come.

Gareth sighed and looked around. Not much here for entertainment. He'd like to explore the city but doubted that the others would look favorably on that suggestion.

"Anybody got a deck of cards?"

His question was met by a pair of glowing glares.

Yes, it was definitely going to be a long three days.

CHAPTER 6

L ady White had lost all sense of time and direction as she walked along the seemingly endless, identical tunnels running under the desert. Since the ghoul pit, she hadn't seen or sensed anything, living or dead. Only a vague feeling of dread that hung over everything. If she'd been human, she would have attributed that last feeling to the corruption that filled the ether. But she had long since gotten over her discomfort and now drew strength from the darkness.

No, whatever she sensed, it wasn't just a lingering effect of corruption. Something was down here. Something that wanted her crushed. It felt different from the guardian she faced on the surface. More primitive and savage.

She shook her head. Whatever it was, she had no illusions about getting out of these tunnels without facing it.

A tingle in the back of her mind alerted her that her warbeast wanted something. Despite its bestial appearance, the demon she bound was reasonably intelligent. Not brilliant like some of the greater demons she'd spoken with over the years, but smart enough.

Lady White closed her eyes and strengthened the connection until she could see through the beast's eyes. The blinding brightness of the noonday sun made her flinch. Once she got used to it, she focused on what had her beast so interested. Far in the distance, a flash of silver glittered.

Using a little more of her power, she enhanced its vision. A slow smile spread across her lips. That was the portal she sought. The tops of three pyramids were also visible. Looked like these tunnels were taking her exactly where she wanted to go. That was some consolation at least. She offered her beast a psychic pat on the head and returned her focus to her body.

The flatness of the desert made distances hard to judge. Her best guess was that she still had hundreds of miles to cover. But at least her goal was in sight.

Heartened, she set out again at a brisk pace. Her legs offered no complaints despite having been walking for possibly weeks nonstop. One of the many advantages of an undead body. Even better, her magic had nearly returned to full strength. She didn't dare call on Astaroth directly again, but the rest of her abilities should work fine.

It wasn't that she lacked the strength to call on him. Rather, the demon lord favored those with the will to overcome their enemies on their own. Weaklings that constantly needed their hand held would receive no favor, in this world or the next.

More time passed and as she traveled, the sense of dread grew ever stronger. Whatever force wanted her gone, she was getting closer to it by the step.

The tunnel ended at yet another cavern, this one larger than the first and happily not filled with angry, hungry ghouls. In fact, it looked empty.

But it didn't feel empty. The malevolence she'd felt for the last however long it had been was focused here.

Time to find out what hated her so much.

Lady White stepped into the cavern. The moment she exited the tunnel, the dread grew so strong she nearly fled back the way she'd come. Considering magical fear couldn't affect her undead mind, her reaction had to be an instinctive reflex away from the power she felt.

Grinding her teeth, she took another step into the cavern. "I don't know what you are, but if you think I'm so weak willed that you can force me back without a fight, you're sadly mistaken."

A blob of inky darkness fell from the ceiling. It reminded her of the darkness she summoned when calling a demon for binding.

The blob slowly took on a humanoid shape.

She debated attacking now, before it finished forming, but the thing was made of pure corruption. Any spell she used was unlikely to hurt it and might actually make it stronger. If she made it a contest of wills, she might have a chance. Certainly more of a chance than she'd have in a straight-up spell battle.

When it settled on its final shape, Lady White was more convinced than ever that she faced a demon. It had black bat wings, spiral horns growing out of the side of its head, and a body that appeared carved from onyx. Its face was smooth and without expression.

She drew herself up to her full height, back straight and unafraid. When dealing with demons, confidence was every-thing. They could home in on the slightest mental weakness. She'd been dealing with the creatures for long enough that she felt certain this was a battle she knew how to win.

"Step aside," she said. "I have no quarrel with you."

"I am the guardian of the underworld. If my compatriot sent you here, you must be strong. That is well. I haven't had a challenge in far too long."

So much for talking her way past the demon.

She drew a breath to try another tack.

A sphere of darkness shot at her.

She conjured a blade of corruption and sliced it in half, sending blobs of darkness flying past her on either side. It was so dense, even an undead like her would be crushed by a direct hit.

Another sphere came hurtling at her.

Lady White leapt aside. Defending would drain her strength too quickly.

The sphere curved, coming back at her.

With no other choice she blasted it to bits.

So far, the demon hadn't so much as twitched. There was no path to victory like this. She needed to close and fight it directly.

Grimacing, she sprinted right toward the creature.

The demon gathered and hurled darkness so quickly she didn't even sense the spell forming. But she did anticipate it.

A shield of darkness formed around her and she kept running.

The third sphere broke and dissipated.

Through the haze of corruption, she saw the demon, still unmoving, ten feet away.

A fourth sphere hammered into her barrier and shattered it.

Ignoring the pain, she pushed through and reached out. Her fingers reached its head and sank in to the second knuckle.

With an effort of will, she sent her mind into its.

———

Lady White stood in the infinite darkness of the demon's mind. Its humanoid form loomed above her, ten times bigger here than in the cavern. No sensation reached her. She felt totally disconnected from her senses.

"You have great courage coming here," the demon's voice came from all around her. "Were you so very desperate?"

She ignored the question and reached out with her magical senses. It had to be here somewhere, the demon's link to the mortal realm. If she severed that link, she could send it back to whatever hell it came from.

"You won't find it," the demon said. "I wasn't bound to this realm like your warbeast. The mighty Lord Amet Sur summoned me body and soul from hell."

Her eyes snapped open. To summon a demon to the mortal realm required human life energy equivalent to the demon's corruption. How many lives had it taken to summon this creature? She couldn't imagine a human lord being willing to sacrifice so many of his own people just to call a single demon.

"Amet Sur and his fellows had an interesting view of mortal life. They treated it as just another resource, no different than gold or food. If he needed the lives of thousands to power a spell, he would claim them with as little thought as a farmer harvesting wheat. Of all the wizards I've met over the millennia, I respected him the most."

Lady White understood that. Unfortunately for her, she couldn't follow her original plan. She tried to return her consciousness to her body and failed.

"You chose my mind as our battlefield," the demon said. "I accept your challenge."

She barely had time to curse her luck when the darkness

closed in and tried to crush her into oblivion. Gathering her will, she pushed back, gaining a fraction of breathing room.

She had no hope of defeating this creature in a contest of pure strength. Even if it was summoned, the demon still had to have a core, someplace its consciousness resided. She needed to find it and quickly.

Lady White dissolved her psychic form and sent her awareness racing through the demon's mind.

Where was it?

"You're a clever one," the demon said.

An inky black bottle appeared and a vortex tried to suck her insubstantial body in.

She countered, becoming solid just long enough to smash the construct. Before she could dissolve again, a bolt of darkness shot through her.

The pain drew a gasp but failed to break her concentration.

Insubstantial once more, she continued her search. The demon's consciousness would be the most powerful concentration of corruption.

She found it soon enough: a ball the size of her head made of pure, compressed corruption. Her body reformed and a blade took shape in her hand.

Refusing to give the demon time to react, she slashed across its core.

Her blade shattered, not even making a scratch.

Not exactly the result she'd been hoping for.

A spike shot out from the sphere, impaling her psychic body. The pain nearly blinded her. She couldn't even scream.

Even through the pain she kept her focus. Locking her arms around the spike, she flowed down it like water. At the base she found a tiny crack in the core's smooth surface.

It was all the opening she needed.

Lady White burrowed her way inside.

"What are you doing?" the demon demanded.

She ignored it and dug deeper, forcing her consciousness through layer after layer of vileness. A mortal woman would have been killed a thousand times over, but for an undead, the experience was merely unpleasant. Like having your brain run through a cheese grater was unpleasant.

When she had fully entered the demon's core, Lady White gathered every ounce of her power and thrust outward.

The core exploded. Shards of corruption flew in every direction.

She blinked and found herself back in her body. The demon slowly sunk into the floor.

"Well fought. It will take me years to reform my core. Should we meet again, I will not underestimate you a second time."

The demon vanished into the stone and Lady White collapsed. Never in her nearly two hundred years had she felt this weak, not even during her time as a mortal.

With the demon temporarily defeated, a short rest should be safe enough. Not that she had a choice.

CHAPTER 7

Eddred leaned back in his chair, put his feet up on the table, and stared up at the bare rafters of his rented warehouse. The boards looked thick and sturdy enough to withstand a Markane winter. He doubted they'd ever seen snow in the City of Coins, it must have been simply pride in their craftsmanship that inspired the builders.

Since he hadn't seen a mercenary in over a week, random thoughts like this flitted through his mind off and on. Just a distraction from his impressive failures. Lord Valtan might have been better advised to send someone else to take his place. It's not like they could have done any worse. Of course, the Arcane Lord didn't have many people to send on missions. In fact, Eddred was his only option at the moment. So he'd just have to muddle through.

He glanced right to find Lilly, the second half of his body-guard duo, watching him with a concerned frown. The creases on her forehead made her look older than her nearly thirty years. He knew both she and Adam worried about him. In truth he didn't know why either of them bothered to keep watch. He wasn't even a king in more than name. Habit most likely.

Uther no longer bothered to show up. But he hadn't gone back to the whores. Instead, he spent hours on deck sparring with the crew. He seemed determined to hone his swordsman-ship to a razor edge. Eddred appreciated his dedication but didn't really understand it.

A heavy blow to the warehouse door startled him out of his revery.

"It's Captain Kane," Lilly said to his unasked question.

Eddred brightened and went to let the mercenary in himself. When he opened the door, he found Kane dressed in the same battered leather armor and armed to the teeth. He'd shaved at some point and a smooth face made him look younger. Given how much Eddred sweated in just his light robes, he couldn't imagine the armor being at all comfortable.

"Majesty!" Kane beamed at him. "Since you're still here, I assume you're still in the market for mercenaries. My men just returned from a most profitable venture. I can have a dozen ready to leave on your mission as soon as first light tomorrow."

"Heaven bless you, Captain, I was beginning to lose hope. Have them at my ship at sunrise. We need to sail a day or so down the coast to a cove we scouted as a potential landing point."

"Certainly, we'll be there. Don't forget, I'll need the remainder of my fifty percent deposit."

Eddred nodded. "You'll have it, never fear."

The two men shook hands and Kane took his leave.

Eddred turned back to Lilly. "Finally! Finally something is going our way. Let's return to the ship. We'll need to purchase supplies for the team and get everything loaded for an early departure."

"Yes, Majesty," Lilly said. "If I might add, it's good to see you showing some life."

Eddred blew out a sigh. "I know I haven't been the best leader over the last few weeks. I apologize for that. The task just seemed so overwhelming, especially when we couldn't even hire the help we needed. But that's the past. Soon enough we'll have the scroll safely in Lord Valtan's hands. Ha! I'd like to see that upstart Otto Shenk wrest the artifact from him."

———

E ddred eyed the mercenaries sprawled across the deck of his ship with a jaundiced eye. Beggars couldn't be choosers and he certainly didn't have a line of fighters beating down his door to come on this mission, but heaven help him. This lot looked like they'd been fighting a war for two years without a break. Their equipment was battered and many times patched, and none of them had shaved or, judging from the smell, bathed, in weeks. He'd hoped they might sit closer to the rail and let the spray wash them off a little.

Hopefully they at least knew how to fight and not complain. They'd sailed through the night and their landing place should be in sight soon. Once they left the ship, his doubts would have to stay behind as well. Besides, if Lord Valtan's device worked as well as Eddred hoped, the fighting should be minimal.

Uther picked his way through the mercenaries, pausing once to exchange words with the group's leader—not Captain Kane, who waited in the city. Uther had explained the situation and maybe they were better off without a fake leader on board, but for what he'd paid, Eddred would have appreciated the fraud sharing the risks.

When he finished his conversation, Uther joined Eddred on the forecastle. The prince of Straken once again had that hungry look in his eyes. Though there had been no sign of him, Uther was certain Otto Shenk would make an appearance. There was no way he'd let them claim the Scroll without a fight.

"You look anxious," Uther said. "Do our men not fill you with confidence?"

"They do not. What about you?"

"I've spoken with their field commander, a Sergeant Hill from Tharanault. The man knows his business. He served in their heavy infantry for ten years before setting out for greener pastures."

"I'm not sure working for Captain Kane counts as greener pastures."

"It wasn't a smooth trip. The point is, he's competent and despite their looks, the other mercenaries are as well. So don't worry yourself on that regard. Focus on worrying about ghouls, magic, traps, and heaven only knows what else."

"You were doing good until that last sentence." Eddred offered a weak smile. "I just want this to be over with."

"Land ho!" the lookout called.

They hurried over to the opposite side of the ship and Eddred could just make out a dark strip of land. Looking at it gave him the shivers. Knowing what lived there didn't help.

Two hours later the ship's anchor splashed down as the crew finished lowering the sails. They were still well offshore and Eddred had no intention of risking the crew by getting closer. They'd row the rest of the way.

Eddred, Uther, Adam, Lilly, and two mercenaries to serve

as oarsmen would go first. They needed to get the barrier up before anyone else came ashore. They loaded only the essentials and set out.

At least the sea was calm as they made the half-hour journey. In the front of the ship, Adam and Lilly had their heads together as they prepared the artifacts Lord Valtan had provided. They resembled three hurricane lanterns. Instead of steel, these were made of mithril and were powered directly by the ether. All the wizards had to do was start the flow.

They hit the sand and everyone climbed out. Adam handed a lantern to Eddred and the wizards each kept one for themselves. Ether swirled around Eddred's lantern until a green flame sprang to life. A minute later the other two were glowing with the same emerald light. Something about it turned Eddred's guts to water.

"The magic feels off," he said.

"It's necromancy," Lilly said. "The flame burns with a combination of pure ether and the corrupt energy that pervades everything here. Corruption and the living aren't a healthy mix. But don't worry, Majesty. While it may make you queasy, the magic will do no real harm."

Eddred didn't feel terribly reassured but kept his concerns quiet.

"You two go back to the ship and bring your comrades and the supplies," Uther said.

The mercenaries clambered back into the ship and were soon rowing out to sea. They didn't bitch, complain, or otherwise kick up a fuss. That was one point in their favor.

"Majesty." Eddred turned back at Adam's tense word.

He didn't have a chance to ask what was wrong before he spotted two bent-over figures shuffling out of the desert. They could have been cousins to the ghoul they fought last year. The ugly things were a mass of muscle, claws, and teeth, far too many teeth.

"Everyone stay together," Lilly said. "The lanterns' magic only extends twenty feet in every direction."

Eddred seriously doubted anyone was going anywhere with those things out there.

The ghouls stopped at the edge of the light and one of them hissed. It raised a clawed hand, reached out, then immediately pulled back. It seemed more confused than pained.

"So what now?" Uther gripped his hilt so tightly the tendons in the back of his hand looked ready to snap. "We just ignore them until they wander off?"

Adam shrugged. "Basically. They can't break through the barrier, but we can't force them to leave either."

"This is going to be one hell of a tense hike," Uther said.

Eddred didn't know how the hike would be, but the two hours they spent unloading the men and supplies were certainly tense. At least no other monsters showed up to watch the show. No one needed an audience of undead following their every move.

At last, around noon, the group set out on a southeasterly course with Adam in the lead, Eddred in the middle, and Lilly bringing up the rear. Since they were the only ones that could see the ether, it was up to them to make sure the protective magic overlapped and that no gaps opened as they walked. Even a small mistake might end up with them ripped apart if a ghoul noticed.

Over the course of the afternoon, the increasingly nervous mercenaries looked left and right as more ghouls appeared out of the sands. By sunset, when they stopped to make camp, twenty of the savage brutes surrounded them. Every ghoul had an almost comical look of confusion twisting its ugly face.

"Do we have a cold camp or does someone want to cook?" Uther asked as the mercenaries unslung their packs and dropped to the sand.

"Given the distinct lack of firewood," Eddred said. "I'm afraid it's jerky, bread, and dried fruit for the foreseeable future."

"I can conjure a flame if you wish, Majesty," Lilly said.

Eddred shook his head. "Save your magic. If something goes wrong, we'll be glad for every ounce you can muster."

She nodded and settled her lantern at the edge of camp. They made the biggest circle possible, but it would still be tight sleeping, especially if anyone heard nature's call during the night.

Eddred actually smiled at the thought. If that was the worst problem they had to deal with before reaching the capital, he would consider them lucky indeed.

CHAPTER 8

When the mercenary finally returned to the warehouse to get them, Gareth had never been so relieved. Three days cooped up with Grim and Grouchy had left him ready to make a run for it and hope for the best. Only the stupid bracelet Melisandre forced him to wear and his fear of what Ginevera would do to him kept him in place.

"They finally made their move?" Jackal asked as Kane approached their corner of the warehouse.

"Indeed, my friends. According to my wizard, Eddred's group has made landfall and are moving steadily southeast. They landed in a small cove a day east of the city. I recommend you find a different location to disembark as their ship is still on station."

"How do you track them so closely?" Ginevera asked.

"Simple, all my field commanders wear an enchanted ring. I told them it offers magical protection, but the truth is, it acts as a homing beacon for wizards that know how to look. I can arrange a quick lesson for you if you'd like."

Ginevera shook her head. "I'm familiar with such magic. Finding them will be no trouble. I suggest we depart at once on my ship."

She looked at Jackal, who nodded without a word. Gareth had noticed the man held his words like they were made of gold. Not much of a conversationalist to say the least.

"If there's nothing else you need from me," Kane said. "I'll be on my way."

No one tried to stop him and soon it was just the three of them again.

Ginevera stood and Gareth and Jackal joined her, the latter pulling his cowl up over his head until only his glowing eyes showed in the shadows. Creepy fellow, and that was a fact.

As soon as they were outside, Gareth took a deep breath of fresh air. How good was it to get out of that warehouse? He couldn't begin to describe his relief. That he was on his way to a ship where he'd once again be stuck in close proximity to Jackal and Ginevera did little to dim his mood.

The sound of voices raised as merchants haggled and offered their goods for sale reached him from a distance. It sounded so much like home he took an unconscious step toward them.

"Hey!" Ginevera's voice snapped like a whip. "We have everything we need on board already."

"Some fresh supplies couldn't hurt. You need to eat the same as me." Gareth hadn't seen Jackal eat or drink anything since they met. Their companion of convenience was less human than he appeared, not that Gareth needed any proof of that. The glowing red eyes told the tale well enough on their own.

She stared at him until he sighed and got back in line.

"You don't have very good control over your lackey," Jackal said.

"I'm not her lackey," Gareth said. "I'm a trap removal expert, thank you very much."

"No," Ginevera agreed. "I would never bother with someone so useless. I've simply been stuck with him since we left Port Settle. He is reasonably house-trained at least."

Gareth swallowed a retort. While he didn't think she'd kill him out of hand in the middle of the dock ward, he didn't want to push his luck.

No further conversation troubled the short walk to the ship. When they reached the gangplank, the captain was standing at the rail looking down on them. He didn't look pleased. Probably no one was ever pleased to see Ginevera. Gareth could relate.

"Did you forget something?" the captain asked.

"We require transport east. Prepare to depart." Ginevera started up the gangplank.

The captain moved to block her. Man had guts.

"My orders were to bring you to the city and await your successful return. No one said anything about carrying you elsewhere."

"I'm saying something about it," Ginevera said. "And I don't make a habit of repeating myself."

"I don't take orders from you. I serve Ms. Raven." The captain crossed his arms and refused to budge.

Ginevera's eyes flashed with emerald fire. The captain clutched his throat as he was lifted off the deck.

Once the three of them were on board she said, "How many are required to operate this vessel? Surely at least one of you is expendable."

She flicked her wrist and the captain flew halfway across

the deck. He skipped once before slamming to a stop against the sterncastle wall.

As the captain coughed and spat, trying in vain to catch his breath, the rest of the small crew came boiling out of the enclosed bridge. The four men looked from Ginevera to their captain. Gareth really hoped they weren't the brave types. She was apt to kill them all and find another transport simply for the insult of being questioned.

Finally the captain forced himself to his feet. "Prepare to cast off. We need to carry our passengers elsewhere."

After a flurry of worried looks the crew got to work. Thank heaven the man's pride didn't keep him from doing the smart thing.

Ten minutes later they were out of the port and on their way east. What they'd find, Gareth had no idea, but he doubted it would be pleasant.

———

M elisandre's ship made good time. Charting a course well clear of Eddred's vessel, they made landfall a few hours after midnight and several miles east of the cove Kane mentioned. Ginevera guided the captain, using her magic to avoid anyone that might note their passing. Gareth couldn't deny his relief at the lack of further near killings.

Having seen what she could do, the captain appeared to have resigned himself to obedience. How well Gareth knew that feeling.

Now that he stood on the sands of the Dead Lands, a chill ran up Gareth's spine. The air tasted of evil. The beach was devoid of life. No birds flew overhead. It really was a cursed place.

He glanced over his shoulder. The ship was rapidly disappearing in the distance. They were going to have to walk back to the city. Hardly ideal, especially if they ended up with as much wealth as Melisandre seemed to expect.

"What now?" Gareth asked.

He looked at Jackal, but the man remained as silent as he had the entire trip out here. Ginevera had her eyes closed, doing something magical no doubt. She opened them and said, "I've located Eddred's party. They're about a day southwest of us. We'll keep our distance for now. Let them deal with any guardians or traps. We can swoop in, kill them all, and claim the prize."

"What about Lady White?" Jackal asked.

Ginevera shrugged. "No sign of her. You're supposed to be a hunter. Can't you sense her presence?"

"I can, but the range is limited."

Gareth looked away from the pair and out over the desert. Four shapes rose out of the sand. The moonlight didn't reveal much detail, but given where they were, he assumed they were monsters that would want to kill and eat them.

"Guys?"

"Be silent," Ginevera said.

"Guys, we've got company coming."

The pair finally broke off their staring contest and turned to look. The creatures were loping their way at a good clip.

Gareth drew his dagger.

"Put that away. They're just ghouls." Jackal raised a hand and the ghouls froze in their tracks.

The monsters fell to their knees and smashed their faces into the sand.

Ginevera gave Jackal the first look of respect Gareth has

seen pass between the pair. Whatever he did must have impressed her. He was just glad the monsters had stopped.

"I've never seen magic like that," Ginevera said. "Is that a power unique to your master?"

"Not unique, but Astaroth is the lord of the undead. Naturally his worshipers have the power to control them, especially weaklings like these."

"What do we do with them?" Gareth asked.

"Nothing," Jackal said. "I'll weave a forbiddance around us. None of these lesser creatures will dare approach."

Gareth shot a look at Ginevera. When she didn't argue or question his claim Gareth relaxed a fraction and sheathed his dagger. If she trusted his magic to protect them on their journey through the desert, he would as well.

Not that he had a lot of choices.

CHAPTER 9

A trio of black pyramids thrust out of the sands directly ahead of Eddred and his team. Ten days of walking through ghoul-infested desert had brought them here. Not that he'd ever doubted Lord Valtan, not really, but trusting someone and seeing the ultimate goal directly ahead of you were two very different things. Between the three pyramids, jutting even higher into the sky, was the city's portal.

The bright midafternoon sun shone off the mithril, making a stark contrast to the black stone and endless sand. They couldn't see the bulk of the city yet, but in another hour or two the homes and business of the ordinary people should be visible. The city would be a ghost town now, like Lordes. He shuddered to think of the empty streets and dark buildings awaiting them. Even though they'd been gone for centuries, it was still a sad thing. Or maybe he was projecting his feelings for his lost home onto this place.

"Looks like our honor guard has decided to leave us," Uther said.

Eddred dragged his gaze away from the distant city. "What?"

Uther pointed at the rapidly vanishing ghouls. Twenty of the ugly things had been following them since the beach. "Guess they're sick of following us."

Eddred hoped that was why the undead had fled. With their luck, there was probably something nearby, big and nasty, that ate ghouls for dinner and would love to add some living flesh to its diet. "We'd best leave the lanterns burning all the same."

They set out again. Eddred's stride felt as light as it had since they left home. They were almost at the end now. They'd claim the Scroll and return with it to Lord Valtan. Otto Shenk would be thwarted in his goal of becoming an Arcane Lord and the world would be safe.

His smile was bitter. No way would it be that simple.

Distances in the desert were deceptive and it took another three hours of walking to reach the outskirts of the city. No wall protected it from the dangers of the desert. Small stone houses just seemed to pop up out of the sand. They didn't pause to look inside, but judging from the size, there couldn't have been more than two rooms in each.

Roads made of flat, gray stones ran between the buildings and led deeper into the city.

"Do you sense anything?" Eddred asked.

Adam shook his head. "Nothing specific, but there's so much corruption running through the ether I can't tell anything for sure."

"Whatever Amet Sur unleashed here may taint the ether forever," Lilly added. "Did Lord Valtan indicate which pyramid holds the Scroll?"

"The biggest one, naturally," Eddred said.

"I've never seen a city without a wall." Uther looked around as if expecting a wall to appear out of nowhere.

The mercenaries just looked relieved not to see any ghouls. Eddred wished he shared their relief. The ghouls, at least, were a known danger. One they were confident the lanterns could defeat. Whatever danger waited in the pyramid remained a complete mystery.

They hiked through the silent, empty streets. The strangest thing was the lack of smells. Most cities were an endless collection of odors, some good, many foul. But here the dry air held little beyond a hint of decay.

Eddred remained tense, expecting something awful to happen at any moment. All around them, the buildings grew larger and more elaborate as they approached the city center. The air held an oppressive gloom. The few words spoken between the mercenaries were whispers. That seemed appropriate given the city was basically a massive graveyard.

When they reached the plaza surrounding the portal Eddred straightened and drew a deep breath. The air felt lighter here. In his limited vision even the ether looked pure.

"Adam?"

"It's the mithril, Majesty," Adam said. "So much of it in one place purifies the corruption. I suggest we make camp beside the portal and begin exploring at first light."

"Agreed. Let's have that fire we've been avoiding and a hot meal."

Eddred looked up at the black pyramids and shivered. No way did he want to get stuck in one of them after dark.

Lady White didn't know how long she lay unconscious on the cold cavern floor. She was simply pleased to wake up and not find something gnawing on her arm. She sat up, delighted once more that her undead body was immune to mortal aches and pains. A few stretches combined with a brief touch of corruption confirmed that she was fully functional. When she reached out to her warbeast, she found it waiting the same place as last time. The beast wouldn't flee as long as she existed, but with demons it was best to take nothing for granted.

Satisfied that she was ready to resume her journey, she set out down another narrow tunnel. She could not wait to leave these passages. Even undead liked seeing the sky and feeling the wind. At least she did.

Oh well.

Happily, after only an hour or two of trudging, the tunnel began to slope upwards. Her pace picked up at the prospect of reaching the surface.

Fifteen minutes later she climbed a set of crumbling stairs and emerged into the nighttime desert. A cool breeze washed over her. Though hardly a hedonist, that might be the sweetest feeling she'd enjoyed in decades.

Her warbeast trotted over and butted her thigh with its head. She stroked it absently as she looked over the now much closer city. There were three black pyramids surrounding the city's portal in the center. The ordinary buildings didn't interest her, but the orange glow from a fire surrounded by the greenish glow of some sort of necromantic flames did. It seemed she wasn't the first to arrive.

Otto wasn't likely to be pleased when she informed him. Not that she had any obligation to please the mortal wizard, but angry allies tended to act rashly. Though he didn't strike her as the rash type and none of this was her fault.

Maybe she should take a look first and find out what she was dealing with. More information was definitely better than less.

Lady White set out for the city. No ghoul, guardian, or demon rose to block her way. In fact, as she passed the first building, all she sensed was the ambient corruption. If the city had guardians, they were well hidden. Those were the worst sort of guardians.

She made it through the city to the edge of the central plaza. As best she could tell, everyone camped out around the portal, save one on watch, was fast asleep. Her skin already itched from being close to so much mithril.

There seemed to be little danger in contacting her partner. Once he arrived, she'd let Otto decide what he wanted to do with the early arrivals.

She reached for the message device in her pocket then froze. On the far side of the city, she sensed something. No, someone. A fellow servant of Astaroth. A member of the cult here meant bad things for her.

Best find a defensible position quickly. Lady White was a powerful magic user, but far from the strongest in the group. Lord of the Dead wouldn't send any weaklings to hunt her down. Whoever had shown up would be a threat. If she underestimated the danger, her long existence would come to an end.

And she couldn't count on Astaroth's help either. In a battle between his followers, the demon lord would grant them their usual powers, but nothing extra.

Basically, she was on her own.

Lady White glanced down at her warbeast. Well, not entirely on her own.

The two of them hurried away from the central plaza. All of the nearby buildings were sturdy. It wasn't like she could hide from someone capable of sensing her presence. She just needed somewhere that would stop whoever it was from sneaking up on her. Her first strike would have to do the job. If it didn't, she couldn't predict how a drawn-out fight might go.

———

Gareth and his companions stood on a sand dune overlooking the city. It didn't have a wall, allowing them a full view of the entire place. A small fire near the portal looked like a firefly in the distance. That had to be the group they'd been tracking. Neither Jackal nor Ginevera said anything. That was an irritating habit of the pair. Gareth had never considered himself overly chatty, but compared to these two, he was practically a socialite.

At least they kept the ghouls away. The few that had dared approach the group were quickly sent fleeing. Gareth didn't even see any magic, but whatever Jackal did, those creatures didn't like it. Even Ginevera had looked on with an appreciative smile. Impressing her told Gareth more about Jackal's abilities than anything he'd actually done.

"So do we go in and capture them while they're sleeping, or what?" Gareth asked.

"Of course not," Ginevera said. "We let them find the treasure then we kill them and take it for ourselves."

A perfectly practical response, exactly what he expected her to say.

Jackal had turned and was staring at another area of the city. "She's here."

"Say what?" Gareth asked.

"My prey. I can sense her in the city. Our ways part here."

Without another word he ran off at a dead sprint toward the city.

Gareth turned to Ginevera. "Unless I'm mistaken, this wasn't the deal. Isn't he supposed to help us claim the treasure before he runs off to hunt down whoever got on his master's bad side?"

She shrugged. "Try to stop him if you like."

Yeah, right. Getting killed by someone that was supposed to be on his side didn't overly appeal to him. "Maybe he'll handle this unlucky woman and rejoin us."

"More likely their battle will alert Eddred and his party, making our ambush that much more difficult." She stalked off toward the city.

Having no desire to deal with any ghouls that might show up by himself, Gareth hurried to join her. "Where are we going?"

"Jackal may have ruined our plans. I want to be close enough to act should it be necessary."

Gareth asked no more questions. Whatever was going to happen, he'd do his best to help her. Not because he wanted to, but because she was the only one on the whole miserable continent that he believed might help him get home.

Of course, he wasn't totally confident of that either.

They slunk along through the silent city. A chill ran through Gareth, so he drew his dagger. The twelve-inch blade would be of little use against some of the monsters he'd seen, but he felt better with it in hand.

He flicked a glance at Ginevera. She made hardly a sound

which surprised him. Being sneaky required certain skills and he'd doubted she had them. Maybe some kind of magic muffled her movements. Gareth wanted to ask her, just to break the unnerving silence, but knew better than to draw attention when on a job.

Finally, they stopped just outside the central plaza. Nothing had changed. The fire still burned, though where they found wood out here, he had no idea. That strange green glow still tinted everything.

"I think we're good," he whispered.

He'd barely gotten the words out when an explosion rocked the city. Everyone by the fire leapt to their feet shouting.

Someone pointed toward the largest pyramid and the group fled towards it, taking their weird green lights with them.

"You had to say it, didn't you?" Ginevera said.

She glared at him like it was his fault Jackal ran off to start a small war.

CHAPTER 10

Lady White sensed whoever was hunting her growing closer by the moment. She'd settled on one of the smaller stone houses for her hiding place. Inside, she found a room with no exterior wall and only one entrance. Her warbeast crouched just to one side of the closed door. Whoever walked through was in for a nasty surprise.

If they took whoever it was in the first rush, that would be ideal. A drawn-out battle against an unknown opponent was risky. If the one she thought was coming actually showed up, she wasn't sure even a surprise attack would be enough.

In the palm of her right hand, darkness gathered. Slowly she collected and condensed corruption into a destructive ball that would blow apart anyone she hit, whether it be a living or undead foe.

Her hunter stopped outside the building. Must be the cautious sort. Pity. Some of Astaroth's followers were more patient than others. She'd been hoping for one of the impulsive ones. Not that she really imagined she'd get so lucky. Anyone that had grown powerful enough to face her one on one didn't do it by being stupid.

Finally, they entered. Corruption gathered around the hunter just like it did her.

At her mental command her warbeast tensed. The hunter was only twenty paces away now. Any moment they'd burst through the door.

Lady White prepared herself.

Corruption surged and the wall to her right exploded inward.

Gravel showered her as dust filled the air.

A barely visible silhouette appeared through the haze.

She hurled the corruption she'd gathered.

The black sphere passed through the figure before slamming into the wall behind. The resulting explosion rocked the building and she feared it might collapse.

Having no desire to end up crushed under tons of stone, Lady White ordered her warbeast to attack. It roared and leapt.

At the moment of impact, she sprinted for the hole in the wall.

An instant's warning was all she had before her opponent's spell came rushing at her.

Darkness formed a shield around her.

A moment later she was blown backwards through the opening in the wall. Her quick protective spell kept the damage to a minimum, but the power of the attack still stunned her.

As she staggered to her feet, the connection between her and the warbeast vanished. Her mystery opponent had killed the creature. That narrowed the hunter's identity down to only a handful of cultists. No way was it Lord of the Dead himself.

The dust settled and she finally caught a glimpse of a pale, handsome face. Jackal. She'd suspected Lord of the Dead would send his favorite hunter. She would have felt honored if she wasn't so scared.

"Submit and your destruction will be quick," Jackal said.

If she was inclined to die quickly, she would have done it back in the Land of the Demon Binders and saved herself a long walk through the desert. A wave of her hand summoned a curtain of darkness.

Lady White turned and ran.

Some spell grazed her side, drawing a hiss. Undead though she might be, there were still spells that could hurt her. And she wouldn't be surprised if Jackal knew them all. She needed space to set a trap. Or better yet, to summon an ally.

Outside she turned down a street and ran away from the portal. She had no idea how the group already here would react to her and had no desire to fight a three-sided battle. Besides, the mithril would weaken her more than Jackal.

She'd barely managed ten strides when he came out of the building at full speed. Jackal would have no trouble outrunning her. Forcing power into her legs, she leapt from the street onto the flat roof of the nearest building.

From roof to roof she raced across the city, not daring to look back, but sensing him gaining.

She yanked the message device from her pocket, snapped it, and said, "I'm in the city and need help. Now."

A faint tingle in the back of her mind hopefully indicated the spell had worked.

She leapt to the next roof and tossed the rune-marked coin off to one side. If Jackal noticed it she was doomed. Her gamble was that he'd be so focused on her that he wouldn't think anything of the coin. Her eternal life rested on winning that wager.

When her foot hit the next roof, it collapsed under her. Lady White sprawled in the dirt and found herself staring up at Jackal.

"And so the chase ends." He reached for her, darkness writhing around his hand.

———

Otto sat at the desk in his bedroom and twirled a gold and mithril amulet. It was a beautiful item, carved with a circle of runes that he'd then filled with liquid mithril. In the center of the runes, also written in mithril, was Lady White's true name.

He'd spent the last three weeks forging it according to his master's directions. Lord Karonin claimed that when he sent ether through the amulet, it should allow him to command Lady White. "Should" being the operative word. While she felt confident in the technique, even the former Arcane Lord had never actually used the magic on an intelligent, self-willed undead like Lady White.

He sighed and slipped the amulet under his tunic. Hopefully she'd never give him cause to use it. Willing allies were far more useful than ones operating under threat. Though he'd made out okay with Allen and Sin. Those two were currently keeping an eye on Jet. He'd grown weary of the demon worshiper's constant questions about when they'd be going to join Lady White and sent her to stay with Allen at his tavern.

The day had been long and his bed beckoned. He pushed himself out of his chair, yawned, and took a step toward the water basin to wash up.

One of his message spells hit him in the back of the head. *I'm in the city and need help. Now.*

He shuddered at the power of the message. Sometimes emotions influenced the force of the message. Clearly Lady White had gotten into serious trouble. More importantly, she'd found Amet Sur's capital.

His bed forgotten and his weariness washed away by excitement, Otto turned away from his bed, crossed the room, and snatched up his sword and satchel. He had the patch he needed to activate the portal near him at all times for when she contacted him.

As ready as he could be, Otto became one with the ether and reached for the rune-marked coin he'd given her.

An instant later he appeared on a rooftop.

He barely had time to register his surroundings when he sensed two powerful sources of corruption below him.

Otto went to the edge of the roof. Below him a figure in a black cloak had its hand wrapped around Lady White's throat and was holding her two feet off the ground.

Not even thinking, Otto drew his sword and leapt.

Ether flowed into his body as he fell.

His mithril sword sliced the arm holding Lady White off at the elbow. He caught just a glimpse of a pained, pale face before the man vanished.

Otto kept his sword drawn just in case the stranger returned. Beside him, Lady White tossed the forearm away and rubbed her pale throat. She looked shaken, even more so than when the cultists had her trapped in the Land of the Demon Binders.

"I doubted you'd come," she said at last.

"Why? We're allies, aren't we? I promised you protection from your enemies in exchange for your loyalty. Wouldn't be much of a deal if the first time you got into trouble I ignored you." Otto used a few threads of ether to retrieve the rune-marked coin from the nearby roof. "Here. Who was that anyway?"

She took the coin back and slipped it into her pocket. "Jackal. He's the favored hunter of Lord of the Dead, the leader of my former cult. Of all those Lord of the Dead might have sent, Jackal is the one I least wanted to deal with."

"Why? What makes him so special? When I first sensed the two of you, your levels of corruption seemed about even."

"He's a little stronger than me." From the tone of her voice, it took a lot to admit that. "The real problem is our specialties. My talents lie in summoning and binding as well as long-range communications. When my superiors trained me, it was to be a leader who oversaw others in the field. Jackal is a hunter. Finding and destroying foes directly is his focus. Basically, this situation is where I'm weakest and he's strongest."

"Hmm. That's hardly ideal. At least he seems vulnerable to mithril. Is he an undead like you?"

"No, Jackal is demon bound. Lord of the Dead summoned a demon spirit, stripped it of personality, and infused the energy into Jackal. Basically, he retained his human personality and intellect and gained the powers of a demon. Of course, it cost his soul, but that's no different than any of us that serve Astaroth."

"How did he escape, some sort of teleportation?" If Jackal could appear and disappear at will, it would make killing him far more difficult.

"He can travel short distances as a black mist, but only for a second or two, then he needs to reform. It's not a trick he can use often."

Otto nodded, that was something at least. "What else can he do?"

"Jackal is strong and fast, his body heals quickly, though I doubt that arm will be growing back since you severed it with a mithril blade. But just to make sure." She pointed at the severed appendage and it melted into a puddle of liquid meat. "There. He can also rip the corruption out of an undead or demonic creature, destroying it utterly."

"That's what he was doing to you?"

She shuddered. "If you hadn't arrived when you did, I'd have lasted ten seconds at most."

"Well then, I'm glad I made it in time. Anything else I need to know?"

"There was another party already here when I arrived. They were camped near the portal."

"Friends of Jackal's?"

"He doesn't have friends. Whoever they were, I doubt he was with them." She nodded toward his sword. "Could you put that away? It's making my skin crawl. Jackal won't attack again until he recovers from the blow you struck."

Otto obliged her, sheathing the blade. "I'll just take a quick look at these strangers."

He closed his eyes and extended his sight. The corruption burned, but this time he knew what to expect and protected himself from the worst of the negative effects. His ethereal construct reached a point far above the plaza. In the distance he caught a glimpse of green light and figures racing toward the largest of three black pyramids. That would be Amet Sur's palace.

The group was a few strides from the only visible entrance.

Sending the construct in for a closer look, he slammed into an invisible barrier right at the palace entrance. The green light quickly dwindled out of sight. Whoever they were, he couldn't follow them in there. The barrier reminded him of the one generated by the knight statue he took from Sin. For a wizard of Lord Sur's skill, forging such a barrier would be a simple matter.

If he wanted to deal with them, he'd have to do it in person.

Otto let the construct vanish and returned his sight to his body. "They've fled into the pyramid. I saw no sign of Jackal or anyone else in the plaza."

"Jackal would have no more desire than I do to get close to the portal."

"It's going to get considerably worse once I activate it. Pure ether charging the mithril should make it impossible for any undead to approach within a hundred yards or so. I planned to use it as a safe zone for our camp. This Jackal problem complicates my plan. You'll be a sitting duck outside the protected zone on your own. We need to find him and destroy him before I activate the portal."

"I like that plan, but now that he knows I have help, he won't attack again. Jackal is too smart for that. He'll wait until I'm alone. We're both immortal. Time is on his side."

"Is it? I assume your former leader wouldn't want his best hunter tied up for potentially decades. Time may be on his side in theory, but in reality, there's some kind of a limit. That limit is certainly longer than I plan to invest in this dead city, but still."

"Okay, what's your plan?"

"Simple, we hunt the hunter."

CHAPTER 11

W hen the explosions woke him from a dead sleep, Eddred didn't need long to decide what to do. They grabbed the lanterns and he ordered everyone into the pyramid. A few more hours' sleep didn't hold nearly the appeal of a defensible position. He didn't pause to consider what they might find inside. At least they'd have walls around them and only one direction to defend.

They raced ten yards down a corridor from the main entrance before he slowed and turned back. There was no sign of enemy pursuit. Good, the last thing Eddred wanted to do was rush into some new threat he couldn't see coming.

"Adam, Lilly, talk to me. What's going on out there?"

"There were bursts of corruption with the explosions," Adam said. "So we're certainly dealing with either undead or demonic spell casters. Beyond that I can't say."

"I tried scouting the pyramid," Lilly said. "But some magic prevents me from extending my senses. We'll have to take it room by room."

That wasn't what Eddred wanted to hear, but he wasn't

surprised either. Naturally an Arcane Lord wouldn't want his secrets exposed so easily. They didn't even know if this was the pyramid where Amet Sur kept the Scroll. Lord Valtan said it was, but the last time he saw it was over a century before he banished the others to the netherworld. That was approaching eight hundred years ago. Heaven only knew if it was still here.

It was a place to start at least.

"Since I doubt anyone wants to return to camp," Eddred said. "We might as well begin our exploration. We stick together, same marching order as on our journey here. Adam and Lilly will check each room for dangers and hidden doors before we move on. We need to be patient and methodical. As soon as we find the Scroll, we leave. Questions?"

No one spoke and the group shifted around until Adam was in the lead and they were all clustered tight around the lanterns. The black walls took on an eerie glow from the green flames. It was the sort of light that might drive you mad if you spent too much time in it.

The hall reminded Eddred more of an underground tunnel than a passage through a palace. There were no decorations, no gold, gems, or art. The tiles on the floor were as plain and black as the walls and ceiling.

"I thought he was supposed to be rich," Uther said. "This place is plainer than Castle Marduke and Father was notable for his disinterest in finery."

"Before becoming an Arcane Lord," Lilly said. "Legend says Amet Sur lived for nearly a thousand years as an undead of some sort. Perhaps he lost his taste for baubles along with his humanity."

"The hall opens up just ahead," Adam said.

A few strides later the group entered a large, open room perhaps fifty paces square. Directly opposite the entrance was an altar made of what looked like solid gold. Black cloth marked with a bloodred symbol Eddred had never seen before draped over the front and sides. On either side of the altar, a shiny black pillar rose out of sight into the darkness overhead.

"Feels like a church." One of the mercenaries made the sign of an inverted sword, the symbol of Branik, the King of Swords.

Eddred seriously doubted Amet Sur worshipped the King of Swords. Besides, there were no benches or pews. While far from an expert, Eddred thought it more likely to be some sort of ritual chamber.

Of more immediate concern was the distinct lack of other exits from the room.

"Lilly, Adam, where to now?" Eddred asked.

"I can't sense anything," Adam said. "There's so much corruption clouding the ether my magic is nearly worthless."

"Same," Lilly said. "I think we'll have to split up and search for a hidden door."

Eddred liked that plan not in the least, but he saw no alternative. "Okay, but if anyone finds anything, don't touch it until the wizards confirm there's no trap. We need a little more light."

Adam's face scrunched up as he concentrated. If it took that much effort to just make a light, the interference must be really bad. A moment later three weak orbs of white light appeared. Combined with the lanterns, it would at least make searching possible.

The group spread out, checking the floor then moving to the walls. Adam stayed right beside Eddred the whole time. The mercenaries were basically on their own if they ran into trouble.

Eddred didn't really expect any. The chamber was pretty

much empty and there was only one way for a threat to approach. They were as safe as possible given the circumstances.

The thought had barely entered his mind when a scream came from his right.

He turned just in time to see a trapdoor snap shut about thirty feet away. A trio of mercenaries were now missing. Dumped into heaven knew what sort of danger.

"No one move!" Eddred said. "Adam, search the floor. Are there any more traps?"

The wizard concentrated again. Long seconds passed before he finally said, "I can't even detect the one I know is there. The same magic that keeps us from extending our senses is blocking my spells. There's no way to know where the traps are."

Their situation just got better and better.

"Suggestions?" Eddred asked.

Uther took a knee and drew his dagger. "We'll have to do this the hard way."

Tap by tap, Uther checked each tile. When everything in front of him passed muster, he inched towards Lilly and repeated the process. Ten painful minutes later, the duo were side by side.

Eddred ran his fingers through his hair. That was all well and good, but it didn't get them any closer to finding an exit from this chamber. There had to be a door somewhere.

He was about to suggest they all move towards the wall when another trapdoor opened under Uther and Lilly.

"No!" Eddred shouted as the pair disappeared into the darkness.

"You aren't paying us enough for this."

The rest of the mercenaries ran for the tunnel. Halfway

across the room another door opened under them and they were gone.

The party was now split in four pieces and Eddred had no idea what to do next.

His answer came a moment later when the floor dropped out from under him and Adam, sending them hurtling down a chute. Moments later they ended up in another square, empty room considerably smaller than the first one.

"At least there wasn't a spiked pit at the bottom," Adam said as he hopped out of the chute.

Eddred grunted, not overly reassured. At least they both still had their lanterns. That should keep any undead at bay. Those unfortunate mercenaries wouldn't be nearly so lucky. Assuming there were even undead here. Looked like the pyramid was empty.

"Majesty, I had a thought. Perhaps the trapdoors are the only way out of that ritual chamber. This pyramid may well be some sort of temple rather than a palace. If so, the lower levels could be a maze to test anyone looking to join whatever religion Amet Sur followed."

"I hope you're right, as that would mean everyone ended up as safe as us. Somehow I doubt we'll be so lucky."

———

Gareth stood beside Ginevera in the now-abandoned camp. He didn't know what she was looking for. It appeared the group had taken everything with them. At least the explosions had stopped. Hopefully Jackal had finished his business and would soon depart. The man gave Gareth the creeps. No one should be that good looking and terrifying at the same time.

He stifled a yawn. A few hours' sleep was probably too much to hope for. He couldn't wait to finish this business and get home. He touched the smooth surface of the bracelet. Would Melisandre release him as she promised? He liked to imagine she would, but deep down he knew better. She'd hold his leash until he was killed on some job or other.

If whatever demon lord he offended would just let him know, Gareth would be happy to apologize. Anything to break the curse he seemed to have fallen under.

At last Ginevera straightened and turned toward the central pyramid. She appeared to have forgotten all about him. Ordinarily that would have thrilled Gareth, but under the circumstances he preferred to know what she was thinking.

"So do we go after them or what?" he asked at last.

"I would prefer to wait in ambush, but some magic prevents me from seeing inside. If there's another way out and they escape, I lose my prize and this trip will be nothing but a waste of time. We may have no choice but to follow them and try to recover the Scroll first."

Gareth couldn't begin to describe his distaste for that idea, but he also labored under no illusions about his position in this group. "What about Jackal?"

"He's found his prey," Ginevera said. "I doubt we'll see him again."

"Ten gold pieces says we do." Gareth pointed behind her.

At the very edge of the plaza, Jackal leaned against one of the buildings. All the arrogant confidence was gone. In fact, he looked like someone had kicked his ass. Gareth forced himself not to smile. Served the smug prick right.

"It seems his easy kill wasn't so easy after all." Ginevera strode off toward Jackal.

"Why don't we let him come to us?"

"He's a creature of corruption. There's no way he'll come any closer to that much mithril."

Jackal didn't like mithril, that was something to keep in mind.

As they got closer Jackal pushed away from the wall that held him up and straightened. Seemed he wanted to put on a brave face. Gareth had seen guys like him before. Well, not exactly like him, but with the same attitude. They'd get a beating then pretend nothing had happened, sometimes going so far as to slap around someone weaker than them just to prove they still had it.

"What happened?" Ginevera asked.

"Lady White summoned an ally, a wizard with a mithril sword." Jackal slammed his fist into the wall. "I had her, until he showed up. While I am loath to admit it, I can't defeat them both. You have to help me."

"No," Ginevera said. "As you so graciously informed us back at the warehouse, all we had to do was find your target and stay out of the way. What exactly did you say? If we interfered, you'd kill us? I have no quarrel with this fugitive you seem so keen to slay. Deal with her and her friend yourself. Our business is concluded."

As she turned to go he said, "I will help you recover the artifact in exchange for you holding off the wizard long enough for me to deal with Lady White."

"You will help me first and you will swear to it in Astaroth's name. Once the Scroll is in my hands, I will help you kill this woman that so troubles you."

"Agreed. I swear in Astaroth's name to help you recover the Scroll."

"Good." Ginevera kept her face neutral, but Gareth refused

to believe she wasn't grinning on the inside. He certainly enjoyed seeing her get the best of Jackal. "Let's go."

She set out around the edge of the plaza so they wouldn't have to approach the portal too closely.

As they walked Jackal said, "The wizard cost me an arm. May I have one of your human's?"

"I'm using both of mine at the moment," Gareth said.

When Jackal looked at him, he thrust the mithril bracelet in his face.

Jackal hissed and pulled back. "Fine. I will find another replacement."

When Ginevera looked back at him, Gareth would have sworn he saw a hint of respect in her gaze.

They quick marched around the plaza and into the central pyramid. A long, dark tunnel ran straight as an arrow from the entrance. Ginevera conjured a light, whether for him or herself, Gareth couldn't say, but he appreciated being able to see where he was walking. Not that there was much to see. A man would go broke robbing a place like this.

They reached a square room at the end of the passage and Gareth's eyes nearly bugged out of his head. There was a table made out of gold in the center of the room. Maybe it was just plated in gold, but either way, it was worth a fortune. The only question was, how would they carry it out of here? He was pretty sure Melisandre expected portable treasure.

"Where are they?" Ginevera turned a slow circle, probably studying the room with her magic.

Gareth wished he had an answer, but he couldn't stop drooling over the gold table. He needed a closer look. His dagger might not cut mithril but peeling gold shouldn't be a problem.

To his surprise it was Jackal that spoke. "That symbol on the altar raiments is dedicated to Lord Baphomet, demonic patron of corrupted earth. I hadn't expected to find his symbol here. The Arcane Lords weren't known for their devotion to religion."

Gareth froze in his tracks. Desecrating the altar of a demon lord struck him as a terrible idea. He looked down at the tiles. A very faint layer of dust covered them revealing equally faint tracks.

"They were here. Looks like the group split up to search the room. Probably checking for hidden doors."

"Since they're not here," Ginevera said. "They must have succeeded. My magic has proven useless. Perhaps the time has come for our trap expert to prove his worth."

Gareth had found his share of hidden doors over the years. You'd be surprised how many rich people hid their goodies behind them. He liked to imagine the look on their faces when they went to check and found said goodies long gone. And here he had an advantage, he could just follow the tracks right to whatever door the first group used.

The tracks led to the right-hand wall. He walked along, his gaze never wavering from the faint signs.

A faint vibration running through the soles of his feet was the only warning he got before a trapdoor opened directly under him.

His fingertips brushed the lip of the opening. The edge was smooth and he started falling. At last darkness swallowed him up.

Ginevera frowned as the trapdoor swung shut after claiming the thief. Trying to rescue him never crossed her mind. The man was an imbecile who talked too much and knew nothing of magic. The world would be no worse for his loss.

"It seems your trap expert wasn't as skilled as promised," Jackal said.

Little as she liked Gareth, when Jackal insulted him, she felt compelled to reply. "Finding magical traps is too much to ask of any ordinary man. I didn't even find them and I made a serious effort. What about you?"

He shrugged. "Baphomet is known for his love of mazes. If this is a temple to the demon lord, all of it will be one giant maze. That trapdoor is likely one of many entrances. Whatever treasure you seek will likely be at the center of the maze. If this is a true temple of Baphomet, there will be more traps and guardians along the way."

"Just how much do you know about his followers?"

"I know as much about them as I do all the other cults. Maybe less than some as I've never been commanded to hunt one of his followers. They have a tower in the capital but focus most of their efforts in the central jungle. Lord Astaroth has no interest in the jungle, so we seldom come into direct conflict."

"Will you at least know what to look for so we can avoid any more traps?" she asked.

Jackal shook his head. "Amet Sur used no markers on his trapdoor and I see no sign of them in the ether. I can't even tell what the trigger is. Once we're down there, coming back will not be an option."

"We'll see about that." Ginevera wove a twelve-thread hammer and slammed into the spot where Gareth vanished.

It felt like she'd struck a mountain. Amet Sur's reinforcing magic stopped her from leaving a scratch.

She paused before lashing out again. Keeping the door so perfectly rigid meant he had to have locked the hinge as well.

Curious now, she hammered a different section of floor with the same result. Moving steadily, she checked each segment one after the next until at last she found one unlocked.

When her construct came down on that one, it shattered the stone and sent rubble crashing down the chute. "There, now we have a way back up. Ready?"

Jackal took a step toward the hole she made and promptly fell down a different trapdoor. Ginevera had barely felt the ether shift before it activated. Now that she knew what to look for, that might help a little.

She transformed her hammer into a raised path and crossed over to the hole she'd made. The chute looked smooth enough, but just to be safe, she wrapped herself in an ethereal barrier before jumping in.

It took only seconds to reach the bottom where she found herself in a small square chamber all alone. A single tunnel led out of the room. So far the maze was easy enough.

After leaving a thread to mark the location of her escape hatch, Ginevera set out to find either her companions or the Scroll. Or better yet, both.

CHAPTER 12

Otto stood beside Lady White and watched her do whatever she was doing to try and locate Jackal. Other than a wavering disturbance in the local corruption, nothing of her magic was visible to him. They'd chosen a spot a comfortable distance from the portal but with a view of the central pyramid. Dawn was still hours away, but his enhanced vision allowed him to see easily through the darkness.

Not that Otto had seen anyone come or go. In fact, it seemed like they were the only ones, living or undead, in the city. Weird, but an empty city was probably the safest place in the world.

That couldn't be right, of course. Unfortunately, the corruption left him nearly blind, magically speaking. It wasn't a nice feeling. The sooner they found the Scroll and escaped this miserable place the better. The tricky bit would be getting Lady White back to the empire. She couldn't use the portal and the City of Coins would be unlikely to welcome an undead, even one as lovely and well mannered as her.

A ship would have to be dispatched to collect her from some isolated beach. He made a mental note to visit Lux as soon as they got home. Captain Wainwright had enjoyed a nice long break. It was time to put him back to work.

"He has to be in one of the pyramids," Lady White said at last. "I can't sense him anywhere in the city, but some magic prevents me from scanning the pyramids. They're like a black hole in my magical vision."

Otto had noticed the effect as well. Some defensive magic of Lord Sur's no doubt. "In that case, I'll activate the portal and retrieve my soldiers. A few score men armed with mithril weapons should make the hunt considerably easier. Not to mention given the size of the pyramid, the search might take some time."

"I'm not certain that's a good idea," Lady White said. "The two of us plus a smaller group of your best fighters would be better. Even with mithril, the average soldier wouldn't last long against Jackal. Plus, if he's hiding, someone with magic will be necessary to spot him."

"Fair point. Okay, you, me, and a handful of others. The rest can patrol out here to make sure no one sneaks out with the Scroll."

When she offered no further argument, Otto took the patch out of his satchel and walked over to the portal. A quick toss sent it up to the master rune where it merged with the portal and rewrote its magic. The whole process took only seconds.

Satisfied with the transformation, he drew the control rod, charged the tip with ether, and tapped the Garenland rune. Ether flowed through the portal, burning away all the local corruption. He breathed freely for the first time since arriving.

· Otto glanced back and found Lady White had moved further away from the portal. That gave him a rough idea of the safe zone it created. About a hundred yards, he guessed. Plenty of room to set up a good-sized camp.

"I'll be back in a moment."

He stepped through the portal and emerged in the fort surrounding the Garenland portal. The night watch didn't appear surprised when he appeared. At this point they were probably used to his constant coming and going.

The night commander hurried over and saluted. Otto hadn't met the man before but put his age at late twenties. Probably a newly promoted officer. They tended to get the crappy jobs.

"How can I help you, Lord Shenk?"

"Send a messenger to Shenk Manor and tell my brother it's time to go to work."

"It's the middle of the—" He choked off the words when Otto glared at him. "I mean, yes, my lord."

A messenger was quickly dispatched and the officer asked, "Was there anything else?"

"No, I need to return. As soon as Axel gets here, send him and his men straight through. I'll be waiting on the other side. Also, the portal will be locked open at my location, so no merchant traffic until I'm done. Be certain to inform the fort commander. There will be some angry merchants and he'll need to explain the situation to them."

The night officer grimaced. "He'll be delighted to hear that."

The fort commander's displeasure didn't concern Otto. As long as he kept a confused merchant caravan from showing up in the dead city, that would be enough. It shouldn't take Axel long to arrive. They'd been discussing the mission for weeks and the supplies were gathered and ready.

Next, he extended his senses to the warehouse to summon Hans. He and the guys were always ready and should be along in short order. The good sergeant would be annoyed with Otto for going ahead without them, but at this point it happened so often he wouldn't say anything out loud.

Otto snapped his fingers. There was one more person he needed to collect. Jet would never let him hear the end of it if he didn't bring her along.

Extending his sight toward the Thirsty Sprite, he quickly slipped through the wall and upstairs to the garret. Jet lay in the simple cot sound asleep. Her pale face was surrounded by dark hair spread across her pillow. She was quite lovely when she wasn't awake and talking nonsense about the wonders of the cult of Astaroth.

Sending his voice along to join his sight he said, "Jet. Wake up."

Her eyes popped open and she looked all around the room.

"I'm speaking to you magically. If you wish to rejoin Lady White and myself, come to the portal as quickly as you can. The guards will let you in."

"I will be there soon. Thank you for not forgetting me." Jet tossed her blanket aside revealing her pale, naked body.

Otto severed the link. He'd committed many acts that some would call crimes. But he certainly wouldn't stoop to peeping on a woman dressing.

He alerted the night officer to Jet's imminent arrival and stepped back through the portal to rejoin Lady White.

———

When the last of the scouts emerged from the portal in Amet Sur's capital, the sun had just begun to peek over the horizon. Otto had to give his brother credit. He'd gotten his people on the move quickly enough. Jet had arrived hours ago and immediately gone to join Lady White at the edge of the plaza. Otto watched the reunion but kept his distance. Judging by Lady White's expression, she'd been utterly indifferent to Jet's return.

Otto actually felt a little bad for the woman. Being so devoted to someone so disdainful had to sting. Of course, Jet only saw Lady White as a means to securing her future now that she'd lost everything in the Celestial Empire. So maybe it was a fair trade.

Hans and his squad had arrived an hour after Jet. They'd simply saluted and moved to form a screen around him. It seemed they'd seen enough strange sights that a dead city and black pyramids weren't enough to draw comment.

"This place makes my skin crawl," Corina said as she looked around the gloomy city.

She'd actually filled out a bit over the past few months and was approaching healthy. She wore her black and gold war wizard uniform with pride. It pleased Otto to see her grow, both as a person and a wizard.

"It's far worse once you move away from the portal, which is why you're staying here with the scouts on guard duty."

Otto expected an argument, but she accepted his order without complaint. Bless her, she really was growing into a proper soldier.

"So what's the plan?" Axel asked.

"I need you to divide your men. I want squads on patrol around the pyramids to make sure no one escapes. Another squad will keep the portal secure. With the ether running through it, I don't think anything nasty will be able to approach, but I want to make sure. Lastly, I want you to join Hans and his men to come into the pyramid with Lady White and me. In addition to retrieving the Scroll, there are an unknown number of enemies already inside."

"That's not at all what we discussed during the strategy sessions," Axel said.

"True, but you do remember what I told you at the end of every one of those meetings?"

"That no matter how much we planned, you had no actual idea what we'd find when we arrived."

"Exactly. This is the situation. The sooner we deal with it and find the Scroll, the quicker we go home." Otto glanced at Lady White and Jet. "Get your men sorted. I need to talk to Lady White for a moment. Join us when you're ready."

Otto left Axel to his task and walked over to Lady White and Jet. They both turned his way as he approached. Hans kept his distance without having to be told.

"We're going in as soon as Axel's ready. Is Jet coming with us?"

"Yes," Jet said.

At the same moment Lady White countered with a, "No."

"But I want to help," Jet said.

"How?" Lady White asked. "You have no magic and no particular combat skills. The only reason you were invited to join the cult was your status within the Celestial Empire. Without that, I'm uncertain how to make use of you. Astaroth has accepted your devotion, but you haven't learned how to tap into his power as a priest. And I haven't the time to teach you, not now at least."

"I certainly can't spare anyone to protect you," Otto added. "Why don't you stay in camp with Corina? One of the advantages of serving the demon lord of the undead is time. You have all that you'll ever need to gain power. Try to be patient.

Once you're actually dead, gaining more power is considerably harder."

Otto felt like a total hypocrite counseling her to have patience given his complete lack of it. But unlike Jet, he had the power to make his goals a reality. All she had was Lady White's dubious goodwill. And it looked to Otto like that was quickly wearing thin.

"Very well," Jet said with a distinct lack of good grace. "If that's where I can be of the most use."

She marched off toward the portal, her clenched fists the only sign of her frustration. Otto watched her for a moment then caught Axel's eye. He pointed at Jet and crossed his index fingers. He'd learned enough of the scouts' sign language to know that was the symbol to keep an eye on someone or something. Axel tapped his temple in acknowledgement.

"Thank you for finding a place for Jet," Lady White said. "She may one day make a fine disciple, but right now she's more of a burden."

"I would have left her behind in Garen, but figured that would cause more trouble than bringing her along. Anyway, she'll be fine in camp. There'll be plenty of time for you to train her into something useful later. Assuming that's safe."

Lady White cocked her head. "Safe?"

"I mean, you're on the bad side of your master. What if Astaroth orders her to kill you or something?"

"You overestimate my importance. Astaroth has worshipers on billions of worlds. He's hardly likely to take a direct interest in me one way or another. It's the leader of the cult, Lord of the Dead, that wants me destroyed."

Otto shrugged. It was her decision not his. As long as Jet didn't cause him any trouble, Otto couldn't have cared less.

Axel left Cobb and started their way. They met up beside Hans and the guys.

"All set?" Otto asked.

"Yeah, no problem. I left Cobb in charge. He knows what to do. How long do you think this is going to take?"

Otto eyed the massive pyramid. "A while. I hope you didn't have plans."

CHAPTER 13

Gareth slid to a stop, his feet dangling over the lip of the chute that had just carried him... somewhere. It was pitch black, so dark he couldn't so much as see his hand in front of his face. Whoever made that trap clearly had no desire to kill the person that set it off. The slide had been smooth and just steep enough to keep him moving, but not so steep that he built up dangerous speed.

What he couldn't stop wondering was why. Why set a trap that wasn't meant to kill? Unless he'd ended up in a cell. Wouldn't be the first time he wound up in one. Unfortunately for him, the jailor was probably long dead. And when he said dead, he meant the kind of dead that didn't keep moving around.

Of course, there was always the possibility that he'd stopped at the edge of a bottomless pit.

He shook himself. Come on, Gareth, get ahold of yourself. At least he was away from Ginevera and Jackal. That was kind of a mixed blessing. A little magic wouldn't hurt anything right now.

Okay, focus.

Gareth held his breath and listened. Nothing. Not a peep reached his ears. The only scent was a dry, musty smell he didn't recognize. It wasn't nasty by any means, just different from anything he'd encountered back home. The air was still, not that he'd expected a breeze underground.

No way was he going back up the way he'd come. That left one option. Easing forward inch by inch he reached down until his toe touched solid floor. Not a bottomless pit then. So far so good.

His second foot touched the floor and he backed away from the tunnel. He froze again, using every sense to try and figure out where to go next. The darkness was absolute as was the silence. He just didn't know what to do.

The answer came a moment later when a faint light appeared to his right. The greenish glow outlined a doorway and the passage beyond. He didn't move. The source of the light might be friendly, but then again it might not. He didn't have a ton of allies. Actually, he wasn't certain he had any allies at all. Ginevera came closest, but he doubted she'd shed a tear if some horrible monster tore him limb from limb.

A moment later two shadows passed the hall. They were distorted by the wavering light, but certainly looked human. Did he take a chance and reveal himself or try to sneak along behind them? It never crossed his mind to let them pass. Ending up alone in the dark again wasn't a fate he relished.

"Hey!" Gareth waved his hands and hurried toward the pair.

The one in the lead drew a sword and shifted to put himself between Gareth and his companion. Now that he was closer, Gareth could tell it was a man and a woman. She wasn't bad looking considering her skin had a greenish tinge from the weird lantern she held. The man just looked angry with his squinting eyes and stubble of beard.

"Don't come any closer," the man said. "Who are you? You're not part of our party."

Gareth had no intention of getting closer to a man with a bared sword. He stopped and held his hands out to the side to show he wasn't armed. "I'm Gareth. My group was following yours and I ended up falling through one of the trapdoors."

"Why were you following us?" the woman asked.

"My employer wants the treasure hidden in this city. She figured the easiest way to get it was to let your group handle the traps then steal it." When the man growled Gareth raised his hands. "It wasn't my idea. She stuck this thing on my wrist to make me do what she wanted."

The woman's eyes narrowed and she said, "It is magical, but I can't tell what it does exactly."

Marvelous, another lady wizard. Where did he go wrong with his life that he constantly ran into them? On the other hand, maybe she could help him.

"I don't suppose you can remove the bracelet for me?"

She started to raise a hand, but the man said, "We don't have time to mess around. Heaven only knows what kind of trouble Eddred's gotten into."

"Adam will protect him," she said. "But you're right, we have no time to waste."

"Mind if I tag along? It's kind of dark down here without a lantern." Gareth gave his best, totally nonthreatening smile.

"You're just going to follow us anyway," the man said. "I think I'll run you through just to be safe."

"Uther!" the woman said. "You can't just kill him out of hand. We're not monsters like Otto Shenk. This young man hasn't done us a bit of harm and he warned us that we have other enemies to worry about."

"You're too soft, Lilly." Uther raised his sword. "This boy already betrayed one set of comrades. What's to keep him from betraying us when he has the chance?"

Lilly got a thoughtful look and Gareth hurried to cut off this line of thinking. "Look, I don't want to fight, kill, or rob anyone. I just want to get the hell out of this pyramid, remove this cursed bracelet, and find a way home. If you two can help me with that, I'll be the best friend you ever had."

Uther finally sheathed his sword. "Fine. As we walk you can tell us all about these allies you seem so eager to betray."

Gareth nodded eagerly. "Absolutely, anything you want to know."

He'd have to be as circumspect as possible on the off chance he ended up with Ginevera and Jackal again. Giving up their secrets would do nothing to improve an already testy relationship.

Life was so much easier when all he had to worry about was avoiding the guards and not getting caught with his hand in the wrong purse.

———

The dark wasn't all that dark when you had magic to enhance your vision. That said, Ginevera hated using darkvision. The washed-out grays eliminated so many details. Not that there was much to see in the empty tunnels. After she found Jackal, the two of them had started wandering down passages and around corners. They'd spent half an hour without finding anything or anyone of interest. At this point, Ginevera had lost all sense of where they were relative to their entry point. Even worse, the thread she'd used to mark her exit had been destroyed by the pyramid's corruption.

She stared at Jackal's broad back. Nothing in his movements indicated any concern. The fact that he didn't need to eat, drink, or sleep probably helped. Jackal could literally stay down here forever and be none the worse for the experience. She, on the other hand, had supplies in her satchel for about three days. After that, things would become difficult.

"Do you have any idea where we're going?" she asked.

"If this maze was built as a temple of Baphomet, we'll find what we seek in the center. I'm trying as best I can to guide us to that point. Whoever designed this maze seemed to enjoy sending his victims on a particularly convoluted path."

"Shouldn't there be guardians?"

"There should be. I would expect constructs or undead of some sort. Traps as well. There may also be multiple levels. If this is the first, that would explain the ease of our passage."

A multilevel labyrinth filled with monsters and traps. Well, she'd known the Scroll would be well protected. You didn't just leave the most valuable and rare magical artifact in the world lying around in the open. Only the worthiest should be able to claim the power. And that was Ginevera, she had no doubt about that.

"There's something up ahead," Jackal said.

She eased up beside him. The passage was narrow and they were nearly hip to hip. Her darkvision revealed nothing. Whatever it was, it lay beyond the range of her sight. "Can you tell what?"

"It's not alive. Probably a statue. My main concern is whether it's just a statue or a construct waiting for us to pass to strike. Can your magic flush it out? My talents lie in more direct confrontations."

She considered the problem then conjured a ten-thread tentacle. Maybe if she probed it, the statue would react. Or maybe something more direct. The tip of the tentacle shifted into a curved blade. If the statue was nothing but stone, she'd cut it in half with no trouble.

Ginevera moved close enough that she could actually see the statue herself. It looked vaguely like a minotaur. The bull's head lacked horns, but otherwise it fit the description.

Her construct lashed out, striking the statue at the waist and cutting it in half with minimal resistance. "That was easy."

A vibration ran through the floor and a wall sprang up behind them, sealing the passage. When she tried to cut an opening in the stone, her ethereal blade bounced off without making a scratch. No going back now.

"Did we do the right thing, or the wrong thing?" she asked.

"The answer to that depends on what happens next. We might as well keep moving."

They walked past the bisected statue and nothing attacked them. So far so good.

A little ways ahead they came to a T-intersection. Nothing but empty darkness in either direction. "Which way?"

Jackal turned left without hesitation. Whether he knew something about mazes dedicated to Baphomet or he was just guessing, Ginevera couldn't say. But since she had no better ideas, she followed along without comment.

Sometime later—it was incredibly difficult to judge time in the darkness—a faint green light appeared in the distance. It looked very much like the light from the lanterns their targets had been carrying. Three wavering shadows passed the end of the tunnel before disappearing out of sight.

"It seems we weren't the only ones to survive the drop," Ginevera said. "Did you get a good look at them?"

"No. Those lanterns are designed to turn away those of us who draw on the power of corruption. If we attack, I will be of almost no help. From a distance, I hadn't realized how powerful the magic was. Clearly they were made by the Arcane Lord."

Even three against one Ginevera liked her chances against most opponents, but if they had any other magic supplied by Lord Valtan, she might be in serious trouble. "Let's follow them and see what happens."

Without a word, Jackal set out after the unknown trio. Hopefully they would lead her right to the Scroll. And if not, she hoped they at least tripped a trap or two before dying.

CHAPTER 14

"**A** demon lord?" Otto stared at the strange markings covering the altar cloth in his conjured light. Lady White had just finished explaining to him what the design meant. "Are you certain?"

"I may not be an expert in everything, but when it comes to demons, I'm confident in my knowledge," she said.

Since Otto knew almost nothing about demons, he was hardly in a position to argue. But finding an altar dedicated to a demon lord in the heart of an Arcane Lord's palace was beyond strange. In his experience with Lord Karonin, they had nothing but disdain for anyone that worshiped a higher power. If Lord Sur was actually a demon worshipper, it would change everything he understood about the immortal wizards.

Of more pressing interest was the hole someone had smashed in the floor. He'd examined it from the entrance and it appeared to lead underground. Given the lack of other exits, it had to be the only way out.

Everything about this situation felt wrong to Otto. His every instinct said they should fall back and reassess. On the other hand, this was the place Lord Karonin had told him about, he felt certain. The only thing out of place was the altar.

"How could I be so stupid." Lord Sur was having a laugh at them. He laid a hand on Lady White's arm. "Move behind me."

When she'd gotten out of the way, Otto conjured a blade of ether.

"What are you doing?" Lady White asked, the horror in her voice clear.

Otto ignored her and slammed the blade into the altar top. The construct sliced easily through the thin layer of gold and the dark stone beneath. The two halves crashed left and right, revealing a vertical tube running straight into the darkness.

"How did you know that was there?" Axel asked.

Everyone was staring at him, waiting for an explanation. "I didn't know for sure, but Arcane Lords were the most powerful humans to ever live. And the most arrogant. There's no way the mightiest would bow before anything, even one of the lords of hell. That meant the altar had to be a fake. Lord Baphomet could hardly be angered by the destruction of an unconsecrated altar. And if the altar was a fake, it had to serve some other purpose. The only thing I could think of was that it hid something. That it turned out to be a vertical shaft surprised me as well."

"Then what are we waiting for?" Hans took a step toward the doorway.

Otto caught him before he stepped onto the tiles. "See that big hole over there? Where there's one there might be more. Follow me, step where I step and nowhere else. I am not losing anyone on this mission, understand?"

Hans's face was pale and strained in the magical light. "Yes, Lord Shenk."

He moved back and Otto formed a two-foot-wide platform

of ether connecting the entrance to the edge of the tunnel. A little extra effort made the construct glow faintly with a pale-blue light.

Otto went across first followed by Hans, Lady White, Axel, and the rest of the guys. At the lip of the tube, he sent a light down. It went a long ways down. At least the ladder built into the side of the tube appeared solid. You didn't exactly have to worry about rust in this dry air.

Much as he hated to send anyone down first, he waved Hans forward. Otto had to maintain the platform for the others and would descend last. When the last squad member had begun climbing, he let the platform fade.

A little tingle tickled the back of his mind, kind of like when he received a magical message. A faint sense of approval filled him. Weird.

He put the bizarre sensation out of his mind and focused on climbing. The rungs were a comfortable distance apart and had flat surfaces making for secure footing. And a good thing too. He lost track of how far they'd gone at three hundred.

At last Hans's voice echoed up from below. "I've reached the bottom, Lord Shenk."

Thank heaven. "What do you see? Is the Scroll there?"

"Maybe."

"What the hell does maybe mean? This is a yes or no question."

"You'll see in a minute," Hans said.

Otto muttered unkind things about his bodyguard and kept climbing. After an interminable climb, he reached the bottom and understood. The shaft led to a massive circular chamber, its walls covered with bookshelves filled with every manner of written material imaginable. Hundreds of shelves held scrolls, books, loose sheets of parchment, and clay tablets.

There were even what looked like strips of bark with writing on them.

A single door made of black wood with mithril inlays led out of the library. The round handle was also made out of the silvery metal which argued that Lord Sur hadn't wanted any of his undead servants accessing that room. The surprise was that he wanted them accessing this one. Though given the altar hiding the entrance and the lack of undead upstairs, maybe there was no other way for them to reach it.

He'd imagined Lord Karonin had the largest library in the world hidden in her armory. But this put her collection to shame. If Otto spent twenty lifetimes here, he still wouldn't put a dent in the collection. It was his idea of heaven.

The strange thing was the center of the room. It was empty. You'd think there'd be a table and chair at least. Or maybe more bookcases. Seemed like a waste of space.

"That's one hell of a lot of books," Axel said in typically blunt Shenk fashion.

"So it is." Otto grinned.

Even if his search didn't end here, this room was a treasure beyond anything he'd ever dreamed. He made a mental note to mark this room with a rune. Assuming the wards would allow him to become one with the ether and come and go as he pleased. He wasn't counting on it, but he could hope, right?

"Let's check behind the door," Otto said.

Hans and his men pulled their mithril swords, drawing an annoyed hiss from Lady White. Axel followed suit and reached for the handle. He tugged it, frowned, and pushed. The door opened inward revealing a round chamber with six archways. Other than dust, the room was empty.

Otto strode through and conjured another light. Beyond each of the archways was a staircase leading up. He frowned.

The level above had to be directly under the altar chamber. That was where both groups that had gone ahead of them ended up. Assuming he was correct, that meant they would eventually all find their way down here, assuming whatever dangers Lord Sur had left behind didn't kill them all.

That put Otto and his companions in a good position. They were free to search the library while waiting for their enemies to show up.

"We need lookouts for this room," Otto said. "At the first sign of anyone coming, let us know. Everyone else back in the library."

Hans pointed at two of his squad members, but Lady White said, "I'll stay behind. Jackal's magic will make it difficult for anyone else to detect him approaching."

"Much obliged, ma'am," Hans said. "Lute, keep the lady company."

The youngest man on the squad paled, drawing a laugh from Lady White. "Don't worry, I don't bite. Usually."

Lute shot an imploring look at Otto who smiled faintly. "She's joking. Relax, we're all on the same team here. But if it makes you feel better, we'll leave the door open."

That drew a round of laughs from the other squad members. They were the first real laughs they'd shared since arriving in the dead city. A little break in the tension was a good thing. Otto suspected they'd all need to be at their best before they got out of here.

CHAPTER 15

E ddred wasn't going to lie, at least not to himself. The endless dark halls were giving him the creeps. He and Adam had made so many turns that he no longer had the slightest idea where they stood in relationship to the chute where they arrived. They had also seen no sign of any of the mercenaries or Lilly and Uther. They might have been alone in the world down here.

"Do you have the slightest idea where we're going?" Eddred asked.

"Not really, Majesty. I'm simply taking every left and hoping for the best. At least we haven't come to a dead end."

If that was what passed for good news, they were really in trouble.

As if to put an exclamation point on his dark thought, a scream echoed down the passage. It sounded like a man. One of the mercenaries maybe.

A second scream was quickly cut off. Definitely not a good sign.

"Do we investigate, Majesty?" Adam asked.

"It sounded like the scream came from ahead of us," Eddred said. "Unless we want to turn back, I don't think we have any other choice."

Eddred laid a hand on the hilt of his sword but thought better of drawing it. He wasn't much of a swordsman at the best of times. His battle with the ghoul last year made it perfectly clear that against supernatural threats, mundane steel, no matter how fine, was of little use. He really should have invested in a mithril blade, but never really thought of himself as a fighter.

That was a decision he'd come to regret many times during this conflict.

They kept pushing forward, more slowly now. After the screams, the silence seemed even more leaden. A few minutes of walking brought them to a small chamber, the first they'd encountered since entering the tunnels.

Adam raised the lantern to give them a better look.

Eddred wished he hadn't. Three bodies lay on the stone floor. They'd been mangled almost beyond recognition. Only modestly intact strips of cloth from one of their tunics showing a black sword confirmed it was the mercenaries. Probably the first group given the number.

On the opposite wall Eddred spotted a square opening identical to the one that dumped him and Adam into the maze.

Adam set his lantern on the floor and bent to take a closer look at the bodies. He didn't actually touch them, thank heaven.

"Ghouls, you think?" Eddred asked.

"Doubtful. If it was ghouls, more of the bodies would be gone, eaten or dragged off. Despite their condition, everything seems to be here save one important component, the blood."

"I've read about vampires, but never saw anything about

them doing anything like"—Eddred gave a disgusted wave at the remains—"this."

"Amet Sur was a master necromancer. Whatever's down here could be something entirely new. Whatever it is, if it's a creature of corruption, our lanterns will keep it at bay. Unless there's something else you wish to see, we should move on." Adam straightened and collected his lantern. "It's a fair hike back to the last intersection."

It felt wrong to just leave the unfortunate men lying on the floor. They weren't proper Markane soldiers, but they had agreed to serve under Eddred's command, so he felt at least somewhat responsible for what happened to them.

He shook his head and joined Adam at the entrance. The dead were beyond his help. Eddred offered a silent prayer to any listening angel that they would be at peace. He would also add them to the list of men whose death lay on his conscience.

"Let's go. The sooner we're out of here, the better."

———

Ginevera and Jackal had been following the trio carrying a green lantern for some time now. The group had been talking nonstop, but they were too far away to hear what they said. Normally she could simply use magic to listen in, but the pyramid's magic prevented that as well. Even keeping their distance, she'd noticed her companion looking a bit worse for wear.

Jackal didn't complain. Showing any hint of weakness would be anathema to someone like him. But that didn't keep Ginevera from noticing. Hopefully, whatever his problem was, it wouldn't prevent him from fulfilling his promise. Assuming, that was, that they ever actually found the Scroll.

A faint ripple ran through the ether.

Jackal lunged past her and grabbed a handful of darkness, for lack of a better word, and hurled it across the hallway.

It started to melt into the stone, but he quickly grabbed it again and ripped it back out.

"What is it?" Ginevera asked. She thought of herself as an expert on monsters, but she'd never heard of anything like this.

"Some sort of undead. It's basically liquid corruption with at least rudimentary intelligence."

"Rudimentary intelligence!" The darkness shifted, taking on a nearly humanoid shape. Only its head was off, resembling a melted candle. "I'll have you know, sir, that I am the guardian of the maze and the most intelligent being either of you is likely to ever encounter."

"If you're so smart, why did you try and attack us?" Jackal asked. "You must know you have no hope of defeating me."

"And I'm the one with rudimentary intelligence? You are trespassers. I am the guardian of the maze." The guardian spoke the short sentences slowly as though to a dimwitted child. "My very nature requires me to try and kill you both. I very capably killed two other groups. Their blood was delicious. Another two groups are protected by some magic that prevents me from attacking. You two were the only remaining option."

"What do you want to do with it?" Ginevera asked.

"I think we should help this poor creature," Jackal said to her complete shock. "It has a job to do after all. In exchange, perhaps it would be willing to forgo attacking us until all the other intruders are dealt with?"

"The magic binding me to this maze requires that I kill all the intruders but does not specify the order." It turned its misshapen head towards first Ginevera then Jackal. If it had eyes, she couldn't pick them out of the overall darkness. "I accept your terms but understand that if you are still here after the last of them is dead, I will be forced to attack you."

"And I will be forced to destroy you," Jackal replied.

"Yes, of course," the guardian said. "That covers all the necessary threats. Now, how can you help me break through the magic protecting them? We need to hurry as the door to the lower nexus isn't far ahead."

Ginevera perked up at that. "What's down there?"

"I have no idea. It's outside the maze."

The creature's limitations were becoming very clear. Much as she would have liked to know more about what lay ahead of them, it would seem she was doomed to disappointment.

"I believe I can deactivate the lantern from a safe distance," she said. "But you'll need to strike quickly as I have no idea how long it might take for them to turn it back on."

"Never fear," the creature said. "I'm very efficient in my work. I'll have them well and truly murdered in no time."

Ginevera swallowed a sigh. If she'd had to deal with this thing on a regular basis, she might go mad. Luckily, she planned to be out of this place and on her way home with the Scroll long before then.

When the first faint scream reached them, Gareth was even happier that he'd had the good fortune to stumble across his new companions. Hopefully, if whatever attacked that unfortunate fellow attacked them, Gareth could escape while Uther and Lilly fought it. He'd told them everything he dared about Jackal and Ginevera. But he'd been far freer with details about Melisandre and the mission. He owed that bitch nothing.

As he'd spoken, Uther got angrier and angrier. Gareth wouldn't have wanted to be in Captain Kane's shoes when Uther returned to the City of Coins. He was liable to end up gutted and thrown in the harbor. Somehow Gareth doubted claiming the lack of a no-betrayal clause in the contract would save him.

That was assuming they actually made it back to the city. So far, they'd seen nothing that looked like a way out of this maze. Wouldn't it be too cruel to make a maze with no way out? What little he knew about this Arcane Lord suggested too much cruelty wasn't something he would have worried about. Hell, he might have just made the place to kill a decade or two. It wasn't like he was short on time.

"There's something up ahead," Lilly said. "I can't make out exactly what, but I think it's a door."

"Maybe it's the exit," Gareth said.

"We're not that lucky," Uther muttered. "Might as well take a look anyway."

They'd barely taken another step when the lantern went out.

Gareth drew his dagger. In the absolute darkness he had no idea what to stab. Lashing out at random was more apt to hit Uther or Lilly and he didn't even know if there was a danger. Maybe the stupid lantern ran out of fuel.

There was a pained shout and a bright white light exploded to life.

Some sort of black blob had bitten into Uther's shoulder. He flailed around, trying to rip it off.

Gareth glanced at Lilly who had her face scrunched up in

concentration. What was missing was lightning or fire or some other magic to blast that thing off of Uther.

Running would do Gareth little good as he had no idea where to go and no light to take with him. Probably the best thing to do was help out and try to win the goodwill of his companions.

He lunged and stabbed downward, impaling the black thing up to the hilt.

It made no noise, but kind of melted off Uther and into the floor out of sight. By some miracle, Uther's shoulder had only a shallow cut.

A moment later the lantern's green glow filled the hall. Lilly knelt beside it, gasping for breath. Whatever she'd been doing must have taken a lot out of her.

"What was that thing?" Uther asked.

"An undead or demon of some sort," Lilly said between heavy breaths. "Nothing I'm familiar with, but its aura of corruption was unmistakable. It's probably what caused those screams we heard earlier. Without a lantern for protection, no one would stand a chance against it."

"Speaking of the lantern," Uther said. "What happened to it?"

Lilly straightened and picked it up. "Something cut off the flow of ether right before that thing struck. There's a wizard down here and not a friendly one."

Uther glared at Gareth like it was his fault. "Your friends?"

Gareth shrugged. It might have been Ginevera, she was certainly powerful enough. Jackal would probably have the same problem with the lantern as that creature did.

"What I can't figure out is why your dagger affected it," Lilly said. "It had no physical substance, yet your blade cut it. I felt the damage through the ether."

"I don't know what to tell you," Gareth said with total honesty. "My dagger can cut through just about anything except mithril." He gave the bracelet a bitter look. "I guess that includes monsters made out of darkness. What do you guys think about going through the door before that monster comes back?"

"It won't come back as long as the lantern is burning and I've placed a barrier around it to keep anyone from snuffing it out a second time."

Gareth seriously doubted Lilly was strong enough to stop Ginevera should she decide to put out her full effort. "Great, but the door is pretty much our only way forward, right?"

"Yes, but I need to bind Uther's wound and make sure no curse or other enchantment has taken hold. I only need a few minutes."

"If you're so anxious," Uther said as he dragged his tunic over his head. "Go take a look by yourself."

Gareth considered his options. The door was just at the edge of the lantern's light, so he should be safe enough. And his dagger hurt the thing. Hopefully it wouldn't be eager for a second fight. Last but hardly least, he really wanted out of this maze.

"A little scouting couldn't hurt," Gareth said.

He jogged down the hall and knelt in front of the door. Didn't look special, just wood banded with iron with a simple round pull. You'd find the same sort of door pretty much anywhere. The fact that such an ordinary thing was here made him all the more suspicious.

When he ran his dagger around the frame, he found no mechanical traps and he didn't get zapped, so that was a good sign. Satisfied that opening it wouldn't kill him instantly, he nudged the door inward.

It swung silently open revealing a set of steps. Unfortunately they were going down instead of up. At the bottom a faint glow illuminated the landing. The last thing he wanted was to go even deeper underground.

Given his seriously limited options, he started down.

CHAPTER 16

Otto needed little time to figure out that the Sanguine Scroll wasn't in the library they found. Anything that powerful would stand out in the ether like a beacon. Both of the other pieces of the Immortality Engine certainly had. Add to that the lack of a guardian simulacrum, and he felt certain the Scroll lay elsewhere.

The thousands of books held priceless knowledge, at least the few he'd glanced at looked promising. But not the specific knowledge he sought. It was frustrating, but there were two more pyramids to search. Perhaps they'd have better luck there.

What struck him as the most strange was his master being wrong about the Scroll's location. He'd assumed she'd spoken from personal knowledge, but maybe she'd just guessed. He also couldn't deny the possibility that if there was a guardian, it had moved the Scroll after Lord Sur's death.

So many unknowns.

Otto had always hated puzzles and this one was no exception. Nevertheless, he would figure it out, even if he had to rip this miserable city down one brick at a time.

"Lord Shenk." Hans knelt in the center of the library, one hand touching the floor. "There's something here. I can feel markings on the floor."

Otto set the book he'd been looking at back on its shelf and went to join him. "Show me."

Hans traced the outline of a marking then moved his hands aside. Otto leaned over and touched the floor. Sure enough, there was something engraved there. The marks were subtle and so shallow you couldn't even see them standing up.

His pulse raced. This had to be what they were supposed to find. "There must be more. Everyone fan out. Search the floor."

The rest of the squad got to work, but Axel kept his place by the connecting door. For his part, Otto drew his dagger and scraped at the marking. A thin layer of stone quickly crumbled away. Underneath, mithril shone in the light.

It was a portal. It had to be. Smaller certainly than the one outside, but the same principle. If they cleaned it off and Otto ran a current of ether through it, maybe it would take them to the Scroll.

He was so excited he barely heard when Axel said, "Otto."

Otto looked up from his excavation. Axel motioned him over.

Not now, not when he was so close.

"Clean those markings off." Otto went over to his brother. "What is it?"

He nodded toward Lady White. "She just whispered that someone was coming."

A little growl slipped out. Otto would happily kill whoever was interrupting his work.

He walked over to Lady White and whispered, "Is it Jackal?"

She shook her head. "It's a human, by himself."

Her head snapped around to focus on a different staircase. "There are more coming from that way. Whoever they are, they have some magic to protect them from undead. I can already feel it twisting my guts. Everything in me says to run away even though I know it probably won't actually kill me."

"How many in the second group?"

"I can't tell through the magical interference." She backed away from the staircase, seeming unaware that she'd done it. "They're getting closer, both of them."

"Back into the library," Otto said. "You too, Lute."

The three of them slipped back out of the antechamber and Otto shut the door. "Maybe we'll get lucky and they'll kill each other."

"What should I do, Lord Shenk?" Lute asked.

"Stay by the door with Axel. Anyone tries to come in, run them through."

Lute saluted, but Otto was focused on Lady White who stared at the now fully uncovered miniature portal. It was a beautiful ring of mithril engraved with runes Otto had never seen before. Activating it should be a simple matter of running ether through the metal, the trick was figuring out which rune to choose as the target. If he picked wrong, heaven knew where he might end up.

"This just isn't my day," Lady White said. "I've got undead-repelling magic on one side and a couple hundred pounds of mithril on the other."

It would be considerably worse for her when he activated the portal. The safest thing would be for her to retreat back up the ladder to the altar chamber. But with Jackal still unaccounted for, he didn't dare let her go alone. They needed to come to grips with the hunter before he could move on to the next phase of his mission.

Lady White spun around and stared at the closed door like it was invisible. "Jackal's here. And if I know he's here, then he knows I'm here."

The expression, "Be careful what you wish for lest you get it," immediately sprang into Otto's mind.

———

U ther winced as Lilly tightened the bandage around his shoulder. He'd had worse wounds over the years, but never a more painful one. Whatever that thing that attacked him was, it hurt him badly. He adjusted his shoulder, trying to make sure it would move should he have to fight.

"Hold still," Lilly said. "I need to tie it off. Don't worry, the wound looks clean and clear of corruption. It will heal in time."

"Assuming we can find a way out of here. Where'd Gareth go anyway? He saved my life." Uther still didn't trust the young man completely but risking himself to save Uther went a long way toward establishing that trust.

"He went to check out that door, remember?" Lilly looked up from his wound. "He got it open and I can't see him. Maybe he found the way out."

"Maybe." When Lilly released him, Uther stood and pulled his tunic on. "We'd better catch up. Sitting here waiting for the light to go out again doesn't appeal to me."

Even as he said it, the green flame wavered and dimmed.

"Someone just tried to snuff it out again." Lilly stared back the way they'd come. "If you can run, I don't think I can stop another attack."

"I can run fine." Uther took her free hand and sprinted toward the door.

Five feet from it the light vanished and plunged them momentarily into darkness.

Uther didn't dare look back and soon enough Lilly had a new light above them. She tossed the lantern away and they darted down the stairs. At the bottom, they found Gareth staring at a closed door and chewing his lip.

He turned as though surprised to see them. "All fixed up? Where's the lantern?"

"I had to abandon it," Lilly said. "I wasn't strong enough to fend off the wizard trying to snuff it out."

Gareth's gaze shifted to a spot behind them. "That's a shame."

Uther spun, instinctively shifting to put Lilly behind him. Descending the stairs was man with a pale face so handsome he couldn't be human. His head seemed to float in the darkness, but Uther quickly recognized the cloak hiding the rest of his body. The woman beside him, while not unattractive, seemed so in comparison. She held the deactivated lantern and swung it casually from side to side.

These two had to be the companions Gareth warned them about, Jackal and Ginevera.

"Hi, guys," Gareth said. "I've been looking all over for you."

Ginevera's laugh was humorless. "With our enemies? I hardly think so. You're a disloyal rat that would betray his companions in a second to save his own skin."

"Well, yes, technically that's true, but Uther and Lilly aren't our enemies. They're just looking for a way out of here, same as us. We should work together, not fight."

Jackal took a step towards them and Uther moved back a step to match.

"This isn't going to be a fight," Jackal said. "It's going to be a slaughter. After all, I still need a new arm. Will you fight to protect them?"

Gareth was spared having to answer when a green light from one of the other staircases filled the room. Jackal snarled and leapt back, retreating up the stairs out of sight.

Ginevera thrust a hand out at them and lightning crackled. The blast hit a barrier and arced off to the left and right.

She glared at Lilly who stared back, not giving an inch. Uther couldn't deny she impressed him.

"Are you two okay?" Eddred's voice came from behind them.

"This isn't over." Ginevera shot a hard look at Gareth before retreating after Jackal.

Uther seriously doubted Gareth would find any sort of a welcome with his former allies now.

"I'm okay, Majesty, but Uther was hurt by some creature in the maze above." Lilly finally turned away from the staircase. "You need to be careful. That woman is a powerful wizard and she knows how to shut off the lanterns."

"Sounds like we need to exchange stories," Eddred said. "Do you know what's behind the closed door?"

"It was closed when we arrived and we didn't have time to open it," Uther said. "Did you see any sign of the mercenaries?"

"Yeah, but there wasn't much left of them." Eddred shook his head. "What a horrible way to die."

"Don't pity them too much. Kane betrayed us to those other two." Uther gave a condensed version of Gareth's story. "I swear when we get out of here, I'm going to break his neck."

"By the laws of the city, Kane did nothing wrong. It's my fault for not negotiating better. I was in such a hurry, I didn't even consider the possibility of betrayal." Eddred turned to face Gareth. "And what are your intentions? From what Uther's told me, you've been a loyal companion since you joined them. That counts for a lot with me."

"In all honesty, sir," Gareth said. "All I want is to make it home in one piece. Though if Ginevera makes it back as well, I'm unlikely to have a long and healthy life. The City of Coins seems an interesting place. I might try my luck there, assuming we live."

"You are wise beyond your years. This quest has consumed far too many lives. It's a relief to find someone that wants no part of it. Now, shall we take a look at what's behind the door?"

They didn't manage a step before both the lanterns went dark.

In the light of Lilly's spell, all Uther could see was Jackal's pale face as he surged down the stairs. A single, powerful blow sent Uther flying across the room.

He hit the stone wall hard and everything went black.

———

Just because Otto couldn't extend his senses didn't mean he couldn't enhance them. Standing beside his brother in the library, his ear pressed to the sealed door, he listened as Prince Uther explained to Eddred how Jackal and his previously unknown—at least unknown to Otto—allies had followed them from the City of Coins with the intention of stealing the Scroll and robbing the pyramid.

Lady White and the others were watching him with tense expressions. They all knew a fight was coming. All Otto wanted to figure out was the most efficient way to kill everyone in the nexus chamber with the least risk to his own team.

The blindingly obvious answer came to him a moment later. Jackal and his allies clearly wanted Eddred and his allies dead. If the problem was the lanterns, Otto could help with that.

Looking through the ether, he quickly spotted the two lanterns and the point where the ether entered them to power the magic. There was also a weak barrier protecting them from magical interference. It was another reminder of just how pathetic Eddred's pet wizards really were.

Otto wove plugs of ether and attached them to fifteen-thread tentacles. With a thought he sent the spells smashing through the barriers. His plugs cut off the ether and the magic died.

Moment later muffled thuds and crackles of lightning came through the door. He motioned for everyone to get ready. The door was sturdy and well made, but he held no illusions about how long it would hold out against a sustained assault.

He shifted to one side and drew his mithril sword. A few seconds later, a pale fist smashed through the door.

Otto slashed, hoping to deprive Jackal of his second arm.

He was a fraction too slow. The arm withdrew before he struck home.

The magic came next. A powerful wave of lightning that hammered hard into Otto's shield. No way had either of Eddred's wizards managed that spell. Otto had never even seen lightning cast without a targeting thread.

He sent threads through the blade of his sword, rubbed his fingers to gather heat, and hurled a twenty-thread lance of fire through the gap.

No screams of pain followed.

A moment later the door exploded inward in a shower of splinters.

Jackal backhanded Axel across the library.

Otto caught a glimpse of terrified figures huddled around a single green glowing lantern. Bodies sprawled across the floor, but he couldn't make out whose.

"You will not escape me this time!" Jackal roared and charged Lady White.

Hans and the guys tried to get in his way, but he was too fast.

Bodies flew left and right.

Otto infused his body with ether until he feared he might explode and charged.

For her part, Lady White sent a fist of corruption to slam into Jackal. He barely staggered then barreled forward.

As he reached for her throat again, Otto swung his mithril sword at Jackal's neck.

Even at enhanced speed, Jackal managed to dodge. Otto stood beside Lady White as they faced Jackal.

The demonically enhanced human pointed and darkness started to rise from the floor. Lady White's own power sprang to life and suppressed it. Magically it seemed the two Astaroth worshipers were evenly matched.

It was a standoff. Otto doubted he could defeat Jackal in a straight fight, even with magical enhancement. His sword skills simply weren't good enough to best someone able to keep up with his enhanced speed.

Even focused as he was on the battle, Otto sensed power gathering near the portal. He flicked a glance that way and found Jackal's companion activating it.

Cursing the universe, Otto readied himself. The timing would be close, but if Jackal was as sensitive as Lady White to pure ether channeled through mithril, his plan might work.

"When I move," he whispered so only Lady White could

hear. "Flee for the altar chamber. Find a scout patrol away from the portal and stay with them. I'll rejoin you as soon as I can."

Any comment she might have made was cut off when Jackal said, "Stop hiding behind that human and let's settle this. I've chased you long enough."

Otto sensed power gathering behind him and a moment later pure ether flooded the room along with nearly blinding light.

Lady White and Jackal both howled in pain.

When Jackal raised his arms to protect himself, Otto lunged with all his might.

His mithril sword ran Jackal right through the heart.

Otto ripped the blade free and hacked Jackal's head off. If the son of a bitch came back from that, he didn't know what he'd do. Right now, he had to chase after the female wizard lest she claim the Scroll ahead of him.

He caught a glimpse of Lady White hurrying up the ladder out of sight. Good. She'd be better off outside anyway.

Someone bumped him, but Otto couldn't see who it was.

He sensed the portal starting to collapse.

Sprinting for all he was worth, Otto leapt through the light. All around him the ether straightened. And a moment after that it went chaotic again.

An instant later he appeared in a dark room. He straightened and conjured a light.

Facing him, a black-bladed dagger gripped in his right hand, was a man a few years Otto's senior. His tunic was ragged and his gaze darted around as though expecting some other danger to appear at any moment.

While he made no move to attack, Otto figured it was better to bind the man just to be safe.

He flicked his ring and sent out a thread. Three feet from the target the thread slowed then completely fell apart.

Interesting. Otto doubted he had access to mirrorshine, so something else must be protecting him from the magic. The dagger perhaps.

Otto probed it with a thread that immediately dissolved. Yes, the dagger for sure.

"Hi," the man said. "Um, are we going to fight or something?"

"I have no interest in fighting you, assuming you're not planning to help that female wizard claim the Scroll or take it for yourself. My name is Otto Shenk by the way."

"Gareth. And no, I have no interest in helping Ginevera. I just want to get this bracelet off my arm and get the hell out of here. Say, are you going to put that away?" He nodded toward Otto's sword.

"You first," Otto said.

Gareth looked at the dagger in his hand as though just remembering it was there. "Sure. I'm not much of a fighter anyway."

Otto smiled. Finally, someone sensible. "Neither am I."

They sheathed their weapons at the same time. So far, their relationship was off to an excellent start.

Otto took a moment to study both the man and the glowing bracelet on his wrist. The enchantments looked simple enough. A proper application of ether should force it to slide right off. If Gareth wanted it removed badly enough, perhaps a deal could be reached. But first he needed to do a little research.

"Where are we exactly?" Gareth asked, butting into his thoughts.

That was an excellent question. The room they arrived in

appeared empty. There was also no sign of a portal. Otto's guess, and that's all it was, was that when Gareth's dagger entered the portal, it disrupted the ethereal flow and dumped them somewhere other than the target location.

At least there was a door leading out of the room. Better yet, the corruption seemed thinner here, allowing him to use his magic more freely. Just for curiosity's sake he tried to extend his sight and failed. Either they were still inside the pyramid or they'd ended up somewhere with the same protections in place.

Either way, it was a nuisance.

"I wish I knew." As Otto spoke, he sent another thread out. This one passed right through Gareth without issue. "On the positive side, for you at least, I believe I can remove that bracelet."

Gareth brightened at once. "Really? That's the best news I've heard since leaving home."

Otto touched the dagger's hilt and cross guard with another thread. Once more he had no troubles. It seemed only the blade had magic-disrupting power and as long as it stayed sheathed, that power remained suppressed. Perfect.

"I'll make you a trade," Otto said. "The dagger for removing the bracelet."

Gareth touched the hilt of his weapon. "It's been in my family for generations. I can't just hand it over."

Otto shrugged and started toward the door. "In that case, best of luck to you."

"You can't just leave me here." Gareth hurried to catch up.

"Of course I can. I don't know you. So far you've been allied with two of my enemies. Neither of those facts encourages me. I'm happy to part company on a peaceful basis. I have enough enemies without adding you to the list."

"Okay, okay. Suppose I trade you the dagger. I'd need some kind of weapon in exchange."

Otto stepped out onto a familiar-looking passage. The black stone and tile floors looked exactly like the rest of the pyramid. Hopefully there weren't any trapdoors.

"Tell you what," Otto said. "When we get out of here, I'll remove the bracelet and give you a mithril sword in exchange for the dagger."

Gareth stared at him. "A mithril sword is worth more gold than I can count. Why would you give me one for this old dagger? I mean, I know it will cut through damn near anything, but so will mithril."

Otto glanced at him. He clearly had no idea about his dagger's true power. "I have many mithril swords but no daggers like yours. And I have an interest in unusual weapons. It will be a fine addition to my collection. Do we have a deal?"

Gareth thought it over for a few strides then nodded. "Deal."

"Good. Now, let's see if we can find the Scroll and a way out of here."

CHAPTER 17

Hans groaned and sat up. Pain was an old friend of his, but damn. He'd never been run over by an angry bull, but he imagined it felt something like this. When that man, he assumed it was a man anyway, all he got was an impression of movement, a pale face, and then something hit him. A quick flight across the library ended when he hit one of the bookshelves. Strangely enough, none of the books fell on his head. Not that he was complaining.

He rubbed his face and looked around. His men were scattered around the room, though happily all of them were still moving, at least a little. Lord Shenk and Lady White were nowhere to be found. A headless corpse dressed in a black robe sat partway into the room.

He was pretty sure that was what hit him. Looks like Lord Shenk dealt with it. Some bodyguard he was. Hans was rescued by his charge far more often than he did the saving.

His sword had landed a stride to his right. Hans sheathed it and went to check on the others. A cough followed by muttered curses drew his attention to the library door. Lord

Shenk's brother—Hans wasn't exactly sure what Axel's rank was now—was struggling to stand. He went over and helped him to his feet.

"Are you okay, sir?"

Axel touched his side and winced. "I think I've got a couple cracked ribs. Other than that, I'm okay. Where's my brother?"

"No idea, sir. When I came to, he was gone. He did kill that creature that attacked us, so that's something. If you can manage on your own, I need to check on my men."

Axel shook his head. "First check the nexus chamber. Find out if any of our enemies survived."

Hans had been so worried about everyone that he'd forgotten about the other group. He left Axel holding himself up with the wall, drew his sword, and ducked through the doorway. Two bodies lay on the floor face down, pools of blood slowly spreading under them. A woman lay passed out beside a now-dark lantern.

The first man Hans kicked over had half his face torn off. He shuddered and went to the second body. Prince Uther's pale face stared up at him. The prince had a tight grip on his stomach. Bits of torn flesh peeked out around his hands.

Uther blinked and seemed to finally register Hans's presence. "Please tell me I'm dead and we're both in hell along with your master."

"No such luck. Though from the looks of that wound, you're liable to end up there in short order."

Hans left Uther where he lay and went to the woman. He'd seen Eddred's wizards enough times to recognize her even if he didn't know her name. An unconscious wizard was liable to wake up at some point and without Lord Shenk here to deal with her, Hans didn't want that. Killing a helpless woman wasn't his favorite thing to do, but having an angry, unrestrained wizard on his hands would be considerably worse.

As his sword shifted closer to her pale neck Uther shouted, "What are you doing? Get away from her!"

Hans really did feel bad about it. A single, hard slash separated her head from her body. It was as clean a death as you could hope for in this world.

Stepping around a snarling Uther, Hans returned to Axel. "One survivor, Uther of Straken, is badly wounded. If you want him to live, his injury will need binding."

"Why, in heaven's name, would I want him to live?" Axel asked. "I've been trying to kill the son of a bitch for it seems like years. Your men seem to be up and about. What should we do about my brother?"

"Assuming Lord Shenk went through the portal like he planned," Hans said. "He might be anywhere by now and there's no guarantee he'll return to this spot. Given our injuries, I suggest we fall back to camp and rest and recover while we await his return."

"You seem confident he will return."

"I've served Lord Shenk long enough to know better than to underestimate him. What about you? Do you not think it likely your brother will survive?"

Axel chuckled. "If Otto survived our brother and father, a death trap in the middle of the desert should be a piece of cake. Look after your men. I'm going to have a final word with Uther."

"Yes, sir. Can I trouble you to grab the two mithril lanterns? I'm sure Lord Shenk will want to take a look at them when he gets back."

Axel waved him off without comment. Not wanting to push his luck, Hans went to check on his men. Everyone was standing, no one had lost a limb, and the only blood came from a broken nose. All thing considered, he couldn't complain.

"What do you say we go back to camp, have a hot meal, and get some sleep?"

They didn't have the strength to cheer, but their relieved expressions no doubt mirrored his own.

A xel worked his way painfully into the nexus chamber. He ignored the bodies and focused on the wheezing prince of Straken. Uther looked rather pitiful, slowly dying on the floor in the middle of nowhere. Axel could hardly believe this was the same man that had run him ragged across half of Straken.

"Come to gloat?" A trickle of blood leaked out of Uther's mouth.

"To say goodbye. You were a worthy opponent. Much as I hate your country and what your people did to mine, I can't deny that. This would not have been the way I preferred for our battle to end."

"Nor me." Uther coughed and twisted up into a tighter ball as if that would help the pain.

When Axel laughed, his ribs made a bitter complaint. "I suppose you would have preferred to end it with your sword in my heart. Just as I would have preferred to finish you on the battlefield."

"I would have rather killed your brother. He's a monster. You must see that."

Axel had his moments of doubt about Otto, but he didn't think of him as a monster. "He is what people like you and your father made him. He's saved the lives of more Garenland citizens that I can count. From our point of view that makes him a hero."

"You poor fool, I think you actually believe what you're saying. Garenland will come to regret elevating him and giving wizards their freedom."

"It seems we'll have to agree to disagree." Axel grabbed the lanterns Hans mentioned and set them beside the door.

"I have no right to ask this of you, but will you tell my father I died on the battlefield like a true Straken warrior?"

Axel drew his blade. "I will tell him you died by the sword."

One swing later, Axel collected the lantern and made his way gingerly over to the others who had waited beside the ladder. Axel wasn't looking forward to that climb in the least.

Hans took the lanterns and handed one to each of the least-injured men. "He's dead?"

"Yes. Is it strange that I resent that monster for killing him and depriving me of the chance of a fair fight?"

"Your brother would say dead is dead and that he was glad to have another irritant out of the way. Lord Shenk isn't the most sentimental man. For my part, I understand how you feel. Let's get out of here. It's possible I have a bottle of whiskey stashed in my gear. I'll pour you a drink."

"I won't say no." Axel reached for the first rung of the ladder then looked back. "My brother got lucky finding a man like you for his personal guard."

Somehow Axel got stuck with Cobb. He grinned and started climbing.

CHAPTER 18

Otto walked through the dark halls, his every sense attuned to danger. He refused to believe that the portal had brought them to some random section of the pyramid. No, everything in him screamed that the Scroll was close.

A few feet ahead, the hall turned left again. For the third time. He sensed no powerful magic in the area, but with Lord Sur's wards potentially messing with this awareness, the Scroll could have been ten feet ahead of them and he might not know it.

"Do you have any idea where we're going?" Gareth asked.

"Forward." He hoped the terse answer would silence his unwelcome traveling companion.

"Yeah, I get that. But I mean our ultimate destination."

So much for hope. "No, I have no idea where this hall eventually leads. I also had only two options. Stand here and wait to starve or push on. If you have another suggestion, I'm all ears."

"Afraid not. If we were in a city, I'd suggest finding the nearest tavern and getting the lay of the land from the bartender if I had a coin or the serving girls if I didn't. Exploring pyramids is a little outside of my comfort zone."

It was outside of Otto's as well, but then again so was exploring a city made of steel and an enchanted garden. He'd survived both of those and emerged with the treasures he sought. This pyramid certainly wasn't going to stop him.

Yet another left-hand turn brought them to a staircase leading up to the next floor.

Finally, this had to be what he was looking for. Otto drew his sword and started up.

At the top he found a single room that encompassed the entire level. In the center, a rolled-up scroll floated above a five-foot-tall pillar of black stone. It gave off an ethereal glow very much like the Heart of Alchemy and the Chamber of Eternity. It had to be the Sanguine Scroll.

He took a deep breath and let it out slowly. At last, the final piece of the puzzle was in sight. And no guardians, but he'd learned from the altar chamber, that just because the room appeared empty, didn't mean no danger lurked.

Not one to take unnecessary chances, Otto conjured a path about a foot wide and started walking. He looked back. "Wait here until I'm sure it's safe."

"I'm pretty good with traps, maybe I should come with you."

"You fell through a trapdoor in the altar chamber. The kind of traps we're apt to run into here are likely to need a wizard to find them. Just stay here where it's safe." Otto didn't add that if he fell through another trapdoor, hunting down his corpse to retrieve the dagger would be a pain.

He turned back just in time to see a second light appear on the opposite side of the room. A moment later a woman stepped through another doorway. Otto couldn't make out many details from a distance, but he assumed it was the woman that activated the portal.

"That's Ginevera," Gareth said. "She's a powerful wizard. You're going to need my help to beat her."

Otto seriously doubted that, but he had used plenty of magic defeating Jackal, so he wasn't at his best. That said, she couldn't have been at full strength either after activating the portal. Not that it mattered. Unless she'd broken through her personal barrier, she had no hope of defeating Otto.

"Just stay here." He extended the ethereal walkway and strode out toward the Scroll.

Ginevera matched him step for step and soon they stood facing each other, equal distances from the Scroll. Her pale skin seemed to glow in the light cast by the Scroll.

They eyed each other for a moment before she said, "Since you're here, I assume Jackal is dead."

"Indeed. I'll be taking the Scroll. Whether you walk away or end up a permanent resident of this room is entirely up to you. I take no pleasure in unnecessary violence, so I'd prefer to avoid a fight."

"I'll bet you would." She crossed her arms. "I say with complete confidence that I am the most powerful wizard on the entire continent of Colt's Land. Necromancy is my particular area of specialty and that Scroll contains the secrets of the most powerful necromancer in the world. It's coming with me. I make you the same offer you gave me. Walk away now and live."

Otto blew out a long sigh. Why were reasonable people so hard to find? "You're no longer in Colt's Land."

With a thought, he sent a twenty-thread tentacle of ether slamming into Ginevera and sending her flying across the room. She landed hard and slid into the far wall close to where she emerged. His spell hadn't pierced her shield which surprised him. She must be far stronger than any wizard he'd fought so far.

He considered simply taking the Scroll and fleeing but didn't want to be attacked from behind. Given her determination, Otto had no doubt if he let her live, he'd be constantly looking over his shoulder. Besides, he couldn't deny a small part of him wanted to test his strength against a truly formidable foe. Foolish, but there it was.

He was halfway to where Ginevera landed when her counter blast of lightning crashed into his shield. Sparks obscured his vision for a moment.

When they cleared, he remained unharmed and she had regained her feet. A fist of ether flew at him.

Otto dove out of the way and lashed out with an ethereal whip of his own.

She evaded the first strike and somehow summoned enough power to cut his construct in half before it hit her.

He hopped to his feet, slightly out of breath, but ready for the next round. Ginevera was panting hard, her pale skin flushed red. Whatever she expected, he doubted this was it.

"Your power is impressive," Otto said. "But you lack the strength to beat me."

He charged his sword with ether until it crackled.

"Otto!" Gareth shouted.

The moment of distraction cost him.

Ginevera hit Otto with everything she had.

The spell had no particular shape, it just crashed into him like a storm and sent him flying away from the Scroll.

Otto used the power he'd gathered to strengthen his shield. When he hit, the ether cushioned him and he quickly regained his feet little worse for wear.

Ginevera was on her knees, the ether unmoving around her. That fight at least was over.

He was about to give Gareth a piece of his mind when the familiar, hated voice of Eddred of Markane said, "It's mine now. Once I take the Scroll to Lord Valtan, your quest ends. You'll never be an Arcane Lord."

Otto stared at the fool. How did he imagine he was going to escape this room? He'd kill Eddred and take the Scroll from his smoking corpse.

All around Eddred, the ether glowed white. Runes flared to life under his feet.

"No, no, no!" Otto ran toward the rapidly opening portal.

Lightning flew from his fingers, but the ether was too warped around Eddred and the spell fizzled. Otto hadn't even closed half the distance between them when Eddred vanished.

When he reached the pillar, Otto looked down at the floor. If he reenergized the runes, he still had a chance of catching Eddred. He watched in horror as one by one the runes melted away, leaving blank tiles in their place.

A single-use portal? Under any other circumstances he would have found such a thing fascinating. All he could think now was that it had cost him his prize.

"It seems neither of us will claim the Scroll." Ginevera had dropped to the floor, all signs of fight gone.

"Eddred has only delayed the inevitable." Otto stalked over until he stood over her. "I will recover the Scroll."

She laughed, a weak, wheezing sound that held no humor. "You will reclaim it from Lord Valtan? Ridiculous. I can't deny your power. I've certainly never fought a wizard close to your ability, but the last Arcane Lord is foe too great for any mortal, no matter how strong.

"Perhaps." Otto raised his sword. "Whatever happens, you won't be around to see it."

Her head landed with a little plop beside her body. Otto flicked the blood off his blade and sheathed it. They needed to find a way out of this pyramid. Ginevera wasn't wrong about his chances of defeating Valtan. Far better if he caught Eddred and reclaimed the Scroll before he made it back to Markane.

CHAPTER 19

Lady White made it out of the pyramid without issue. Getting away from all the mithril made her feel instantly better. She also couldn't sense Jackal, so hopefully Otto had done away with the hunter. She smiled to herself as she imagined Lord of the Dead's reaction to losing his favorite assassin. He wouldn't be pleased, that was certain.

The sun was well into the sky and she guessed they'd been inside for less than ten hours. Amazing how much had happened in such a short time. The strangest thing was she actually hoped Otto made it out safe. This might be the first time she'd ever given more than a passing thought to an ally's wellbeing. As an undead demon worshipper, caring for others, especially a human, wasn't normal.

Something about the young wizard drew her to him. Maybe simply the fact that out of all the people she'd known over the last two hundred years, he was the first to actually go out of his way to help her. He even went so far as to put himself in danger to protect her.

That had certainly never happened to her before. Even

when she was an apprentice, Lord of the Dead had assured her that she would suffer the consequences of any failure. Was this what it felt like to have an actual friend?

If so, she quite liked it.

Now she needed to find one of the patrols Otto mentioned. Not that she felt the need for protection, but rather to let them know what was happening. Everyone had to be wondering what was going on inside.

Stretching out with her magical senses, Lady White quickly located a group of four humans. Since she seriously doubted there were any groups of random people wandering around out here, that had to be who she wanted.

A brisk walk around to the back of the pyramid brought her within sight of the patrol. One of the men spotted her and pointed. They stopped and Lady White hurried to join them.

"Is all well?" asked a surly sounding man with a beard and narrow eyes.

"Everyone was alive when I left. The enemy's magic made me more of a hinderance than a help and Otto sent me out to keep watch for any stragglers." Not exactly the truth, but close enough under the circumstances.

"Any orders for us?" he asked.

"Just keep doing what you're doing. I'll join you for a while if you don't mind."

"And if I do mind?"

Lady White shrugged. "Then I'll tag along behind you."

"Figured. Come on then."

The group set out at a slow, silent march. Each of the men watched a different direction and everyone appeared tense. Wise of them. Just because the city was quiet now, didn't mean it would stay that way.

For her part, Lady White was happy not to chat. Back home

she would often go days without speaking to anyone, living or dead.

The base of the pyramid was so wide that it took them nearly half an hour at the squad's slow pace to make it back to the front of the structure. They were just in time to see a group of ragged figures staggering out of the entrance.

The scouts sprinted off and Lady White followed at a more sedate pace. Even from a distance she sensed Otto wasn't with them. The thought of him lying dead somewhere inside filled her with a strange melancholy. Perhaps even sadness. Very odd.

When she reached them, the one she recognized as Otto's brother, Axel, glared at her. "Fine lot of help you were. Where'd you run off to?"

She was under no obligation to explain herself to him, but she said, "Otto asked me to flee. With so much mithril-charged ether filling the room, my magic was of no help. I was more of a distraction than anything. What happened?"

"Hell if I know." Axel touched his side and winced. "That pale bastard sent me flying and when I woke up, Otto was gone and the other guy was lying headless on the floor. Do you have any idea where my brother went?"

Lady White took a moment to absorb the fact that Jackal was dead and Otto likely alive. It was the best possible outcome. "Jackal's companion was in the process of activating the portal you uncovered. Otto likely followed her in the hope that it led to the Scroll. He—"

She stopped and stared into the ether. A wave of corruption rushed out of the pyramid in every direction.

That couldn't be good.

"He what?" Axel asked.

"It doesn't matter. Something just happened inside and it

triggered a spell. I don't know what's going to happen, but I suggest you gather all your people near the portal. That should provide you with some protection."

"What about you?" Axel asked.

"Whatever that spell did is likely to be far harder on the living than the undead. I'll find a place as close to your camp as possible." Another surge of corruption burst out, sending a shiver up her spine. "You'd best hurry. The power is building by the moment."

Axel turned to the bearded man. "Find the other squads and bring them back to camp. Double time, Cobb."

The scouts broke up and ran in different directions. Axel and the others limped as fast as their weary bodies allowed toward the portal. Lady White went with them until she couldn't stand the pressure and broke off.

She levitated to a rooftop and stared over the city. In the distance, a black cloud filled the air. Peering closer, she could just make out hundreds of ghouls sprinting toward the city. Unless she was mistaken, that was the direction of the ghoul pit she crossed. The spell she sensed must have summoned them.

Definitely not good.

———

As soon as Axel reached their camp, he shouted for everyone to pack up and get ready to go. He didn't know Lady White well, but what he heard in her voice was enough to convince him that whatever was coming would be bad. Fortunately they only set up the minimum in terms of tents so it wouldn't take long to break it all down.

The bigger question was, how long did they wait for Otto

before they fled? Whatever his flaws, Otto was still his brother and damned if he was going to abandon him in this place. Besides, if he did, Emperor Wolfric would have his head on a spike.

"Do we have a plan?" Hans asked.

"I don't even know what we're dealing with. Until some definite threat appears, I'm going to set a perimeter and keep watch."

Corina and Jet came running up from where the scouts were taking down one of the tents.

"Where's Lady White?" Jet asked.

"Forget her," Corina butted in. "Where's Lord Shenk?"

Axel's ribs ached and his head throbbed. He didn't have time to deal with a pair of worried women.

"Otto's still in the pyramid as far as I know. Lady White's back in the city." He waved vaguely behind him. "She said she couldn't come too close due to the portal."

Jet stared out over the city as if debating whether to go search for her mistress. Axel didn't care what she did, as long as she did it quietly.

"Squad incoming!" one of the lookouts shouted.

Good. The sooner Cobb found everyone and brought them to safety, the better. That would be one less thing for him to worry about.

"What can I do to help?" Corina asked.

"Some food would be great. None of us has eaten since we arrived," Axel said.

He took a step then froze as a chill ran up his spine. A moment later Lady White's voice whispered in his ear. "There are several hundred ghouls headed toward the city at a full sprint. The portal's magic should keep them at bay, but if the

Arcane Lord's magic is driving them forward, even that might not be enough to stop them."

"Forget the food. According to Lady White, we have a small army of ghouls headed this way. Give me one of those lanterns." Axel took the artifact from the soldier carrying it and held it out to Corina. "Do you know how to turn this thing on?"

She took the lantern and looked it all over, her face scrunched in concentration. At last, she said, "No, sorry. Lord Shenk would know how, but I'm afraid this isn't something we've covered."

Axel ground his teeth and turned to Jet.

She immediately shook her head. "I can't even use magic."

"Of course you can't." Axel reclaimed the lantern and handed it back to the soldier that originally had it. "Pack that up with our gear."

Hans had his gaze turned toward the horizon. "This doesn't look good."

Axel didn't want to look but forced himself. A black cloud rose out in the desert, no doubt kicked up by hundreds of ghoul feet. Given the distance, he figured they had five minutes, ten at the most, before the monsters arrived.

Whatever you're doing, Otto, do it faster.

CHAPTER 20

Otto had no idea what the pulses of corruption running out of the pyramid in waves meant, but he doubted they boded well for him. Even worse, when he tried to become one with the ether and escape, he found that avenue blocked by some spell of Amet Sur's. Of course, Gareth had no idea Otto had tried to abandon him.

Much as he wanted Gareth's dagger, Otto would have happily given it up if it meant catching Eddred and taking back the Scroll. Unfortunately, what he wanted and what his situation allowed were two very different things. For the moment, he was reduced to running through the halls in the hope of stumbling across an exit.

Relying on hope made his stomach hurt and he'd been doing far too much of it lately.

"There's a light up ahead," Gareth said.

Sure enough a faint white glow filled the end of the hall. White light implied pure ether. That should mean no undead waited to rip them to shreds.

When they stepped through the doorway at the end of the

hall, the sweetest sight Otto had seen in a long time greeted them. It was a mithril rune circle. A quick study of the markings revealed that it was a perfect match to the one in the library. This was no doubt where they all would have ended up if Gareth's dagger hadn't disrupted the magic.

The weapon was currently firmly sheathed on the young man's belt, so there should be no issues this time.

"Please tell me that's the way out of here," Gareth said.

"At the very least it's the way back to the library where we started. The actual way out isn't far from there. Keep quiet now, I need to focus."

Happily, the talkative young man complied and Otto began to charge the runes. He went slow, both to make sure he made no mistakes and to conserve his strength. Back-to-back battles had left him drained. What he really wanted now was hot food and a nap. Maybe Hans would have a pot of stew going when they got back, though given the situation he didn't like his chances.

He finished the spell and all the runes glowed strong and bright. "Step through then move out of the way. I'll be right behind you."

Gareth nodded, took a deep breath, and strode into the light.

Otto counted to three and followed. The straight lines of ether filled his vision and the next thing he knew, he was in the library. Off to the side, Gareth looked a little dazed but otherwise unharmed.

"Traveling by portal can be disorientating." Likely his dagger had spared him the worst of the effects his first time through.

"Yeah. I wouldn't mind if it was my last time using one."

Otto chuckled and headed for the ladder. "You get used to

it. Come on. Hopefully one of the patrols picked up Eddred, assuming he appeared in the vicinity of the pyramid."

"What are the odds of that?" Gareth asked as they clanked up the rungs.

"Lousy. With my luck he's probably on the outskirts of the City of Coins ready to board a ship home."

"I wouldn't worry about that. Their ship is anchored off the coast about a day or so east of the city. We sailed wide around it when we came after them."

Otto pulled himself up and out of the shaft. He conjured a path and made it glow blue for Gareth to follow. As he strode toward the exit, Otto did a mental calculation. Given the city's location and Eddred's landing site, it would take about a week to make the hike. Traveling by portal, they'd reach home in moments then go on to Lux to collect every ship he could requisition. There should be enough to fully blockade Markane and catch Eddred.

Smiling to himself, he reached the end of the tunnel and stopped dead. The portal still blazed with ether, but something was wrong. Corruption had worked its way into the ether powering it. Just using it would be a risk. Is that what the magic he sensed had done?

Even worse, a black cloud was rising to the south. Otto extended his vision, wincing as the corruption burned his eyes. That, unfortunately, was the least of his problems. The cloud was coming from a huge force of ghouls running toward the city at a dead sprint. They had minutes at most before the nasty things arrived.

"Not to nag, but could you take this off my arm now?" Gareth asked.

Otto gave a little shake. He'd been so focused on the problems in front of him he'd forgotten about Gareth for a moment.

"No. We have more pressing concerns."

Gareth dropped his hand to the hilt of his dagger. "You're not going to try and double-cross me, are you? I hate it when people do that."

"When I give my word, I keep it. At the moment, the horde of hundreds of ghouls seems the more serious problem." Otto gave him a hard look. "Now take your hand off that weapon before I melt your brain."

"Sure, sorry. It's just I've been on a bad run lately, you know?"

Otto couldn't have cared less about Gareth's poor luck. That mithril band was a minor issue compared to an undead army and their distinct lack of options for a quick escape. Besides, the only wizard apt to be looking for him now lacked a head.

They quick-marched back to the portal, arriving at the same time as Cobb and a squad of scouts. Good, it looked like Axel had ordered everyone back to camp. With any luck the portal's magic, even corrupted as it was, would still serve to hold off the ghouls.

"Master!" Corina came running and wrapped her arms around him. "We were so worried. What happened? Who's he?"

"Long story. This is Gareth, he'll be traveling with us for a little while. I assume you know about the ghouls?"

"They just reached the city outskirts." Hans walked over, looking a bit lame, but otherwise unharmed. "Good to see you well, my lord. Did you get what you were after?"

"No, Eddred beat me to it."

"We'll catch him," Corina said. "But right now, we need to flee."

"We can't," Otto said. "Something's happened to the portal. I fear it may not be safe. Until I find the source of the corruption contaminating it and negate the flow, anyone passing through may not emerge alive."

"Will it still keep the ghouls at bay?" Hans asked.

"No idea. Work with Axel to form a defensive perimeter. Where's Lady White? I need to talk to her."

"She didn't want to get too close." Corina waved toward the city. "She's over there somewhere."

Otto extended his vision again and quickly spotted her on a rooftop to the northwest. "I found her. Hold out as long as you can. If it looks like certain death from the ghouls, take your chances with the portal. Otherwise, I wouldn't risk it."

He became one with the ether and reappeared on the rooftop with Lady White.

She smiled despite the situation. "I knew you'd make it."

"I haven't made it yet. Did you notice the corruption around the portal?"

"I don't like to look too closely at it." She turned and stared for a moment. "I see it now. What does it mean?"

"It means I don't dare use it. Can you track the source? I need to shut it down to get everyone out of here."

Lady White closed her eyes and corruption swirled around her. She slowly rose a foot off the roof and spun in a circle. When she stopped and touched back down, she faced back toward the pyramids. Exactly where Otto didn't want to go. He had no idea where he might look for the source of corruption. He'd already visited every entrance and chamber he could find.

"The corruption is coming from the two smaller pyramids."

"The smaller ones?" He hadn't expected that.

Otto squinted but there was so much ambient corruption staining the ether, he couldn't pick out anything specific from the pyramids. Still, he trusted Lady White. Which surprised him, but there it was. The real question was, how did he get inside?

"I don't suppose you can spot a door?" he asked.

"Not from here. If you want to investigate, I suggest we go before the ghouls move any closer."

"We?"

"You killed Jackal. I figure I owe you. Besides, we're allies. What's good for you is good for me."

Her offer might have surprised him, but he wasn't going to refuse. "Alright, thanks."

They levitated down to the street and ran for the right-hand pyramid. Otto stayed half a stride back on the assumption that she'd be more apt to find the entrance.

The base of the pyramid was as smooth as glass. Not so much as a crack gave a hint to how they might get inside. Assuming that was even possible. Maybe Amet Sur built them strictly to serve as corruption generators. With Arcane Lords it was best to assume anything was possible as you'd be right more often than not.

Lady White trailed her hand along the black stone and walked slowly along, eyes closed.

Otto looked back toward camp. The leading edge of the ghouls was only a few hundred yards away and closing fast. The glare from the portal reduced the defenders to dark shapes passing in front of it. Hopefully they'd hold. He'd brought his best people on this mission and he didn't want to lose any of them.

"I found the entrance," Lady White said.

Otto forced Axel, Hans, Corina, and the others out of his mind. The best thing he could do for them now was purify the portal.

He hurried to join her beside a section of wall that looked exactly like all the rest. "Where?"

Darkness gathered around her hand and streamed out to outline a rectangle. A moment later the door vanished revealing a dark passage beyond.

Otto took a breath and let it slowly out. Yet another dark hallway. If he never saw another one, it would be too soon.

He conjured a light and said, "Ladies first."

CHAPTER 21

The light from the portal vanished and Eddred fell to his knees. He clutched the Sanguine Scroll to his chest and fought not to weep. The first part of Valtan's task was complete, but the price had been high. Adam was dead, killed by the pale-skinned monster, while Uther was badly wounded. Lilly had collapsed not long after Adam fell, dead or alive he had no idea. If she was alive, he seriously doubted Otto would've spared her.

He'd lost them all and gained only this cursed artifact. Chasing Ginevera through the portal rather than remaining behind with his companions was the hardest decision Eddred had ever made. In the end it came down to one simple fact. He was no healer and not much of a warrior. Had he remained behind, his death would have been assured and worse, one of those two mad wizards would have ended up with the Scroll.

That couldn't be allowed. One way or another, he would bring the Scroll back to Valtan and get it safely sealed away for all time. He owed that to those that had fallen on this quest. He doubted it would bring him much comfort, but at this point, he'd take what he could get.

Now he had to figure out where that portal had dumped him. Judging by the stone walls and dirt floor, he was in a cave. Light poured in from the mouth ahead of him. He walked out and squinted against the glare. Desert stretched out in every direction. In the distance, the ocean shimmered in the sun.

Talk about luck. He couldn't be more than five miles from the coast. Given his total lack of supplies, that was a blessing from heaven. Now he just needed to find the beach where they landed and some way to signal the ship. A few days' head start might make all the difference in making it back to Markane or getting caught.

A soft growl sounded behind him and to his left. He snapped around and found a gaunt, snarling ghoul staring at him. Eddred had been so focused on escape that he hadn't even noticed the beast approaching. More importantly, why had it snuck up on him and not simply torn him to pieces?

He didn't bother going for his sword. Previous encounters had made it clear that normal steel was practically useless against them.

When ten seconds had passed and it hadn't moved he allowed himself to relax a fraction. The ghoul's glowing red eyes remained glued to him.

No, not to him. To the Scroll. Something about it prevented the creature from attacking. Perhaps it somehow recognized the magic of its creator and assumed Eddred was a servant of Lord Sur. It was certainly stupid enough to make that mistake and he wasn't about to correct it. That said, he'd best get moving before his gruesome companion decided to make a meal of him after all.

Eddred set out across the sand and the ghoul followed a

few steps behind, like a faithful hound, only far uglier. As he walked his mind drifted. He tried to imagine how many had died since Garenland was cast out of the compact. The number defied comprehension. And they could have prevented it all. If Valtan had simply refused to cut Garenland's portal off, none of this would have happened.

But no, Valtan had to allow the illusion that the nations controlled the compact, not him. As if the current group of lying, scheming bastards was better than the Arcane Lords they replaced. The more Eddred thought about it, the more he realized that the reason the Arcane Lords had been such monsters had nothing to do with the magic and everything to do with the fact that they used to be humans.

Give that kind of power to anyone and you'd end up with a monster. It was some sort of miracle that Valtan had pulled himself back from the brink.

When he came back to himself, he realized he'd collected a larger escort. His one ghoul was now six and three more figures were coming his way from the west. All of them stayed a respectful distance away and showed no sign of aggression. He would have happily kissed the Scroll if he hadn't been reasonably certain it was made from human skin.

By the time he reached the shore, Eddred felt baked to jerky and ready to melt. This didn't look like the beach where they landed. Too bad Uther wasn't here. He would have known exactly where they were and which way he needed to go. As it was, Eddred was reduced to guessing. The odds favored west, so he headed that way.

Whatever higher power was watching over him must have been working extra hours as not long after sunset he found the beach and spotted his ship anchored offshore. He'd never seen a sweeter sight. The problem was, without Adam and Lilly, he had no way to signal them.

For their part, the ghouls seemed content to mill around a few feet away, snarling and snapping at each other. Maybe they'd tear each other apart. That would suit him perfectly fine.

He took a deep breath and focused. His vision shifted to view the chaotic swirls of the ether. Eddred didn't need much. Just a flash of light should do it if they were keeping watch like he ordered. Valtan had told him many times that he had a weak affinity for magic. Surely he could conjure a light.

Concentrating until his pulse pounded in his ears and his throat was so tight he could barely breathe, Eddred tried to summon a light. Just as the sun sank out of sight and he was about to give up, a pale flash filled the air.

He stared at the ship and prayed harder than he ever had before. After seconds that felt like hours, an answering flash appeared.

Thank heaven, they'd seen him.

Eddred fell to his knees and let the cool water wash over his legs. He was halfway done. When this task was complete, he swore he'd never leave Markane again. Just let him make it back in time.

CHAPTER 22

Axel stood in the center of a semicircle of soldiers. Everyone had their mithril swords drawn. Behind them, the portal protected their backs. Given their position, it was the best defensive position he could come up with. Maybe if he'd had more than ten minutes and his ribs didn't scream at him every time he took a deep breath something better might have occurred to him. But this would just have to do.

Hans muttered to himself on Axel's right. He seemed more annoyed that Otto didn't bring him along on whatever mad search he was undertaking than he was worried about the army of ghouls even now thundering down the city's central boulevard.

"Does he go off on his own like this often?" Axel asked, more to take his mind off the impending attack than anything.

"All the time." Hans tightened his grip on his sword. "How am I supposed to protect him if he doesn't take me along?"

"What are you complaining about?" Corina asked from

behind them. "I'm his apprentice and he took that pale-skinned witch instead of me."

Axel actually smiled in the face of his approaching death. "When Otto gets back, you'll have to voice your complaints."

Hans snorted. "I'd have better luck complaining to a tree. Lord Shenk does as he pleases and my unasked-for thoughts interest him not in the least."

At the edge of the light, the ghouls had stopped to stare at them, red eyes gleaming. More and more gathered by the second. They were massing for a charge, probably hoping to overrun Axel's far-too-few defenders.

"Want the archers to thin them out a bit?" Cobb asked.

"Not yet." Axel needed to buy time. If the ghouls were content to stand and stare, he wouldn't complain.

"The corruption's getting heavier," Corina said. "I think they're waiting for the portal's effect on the ether to lessen until they can fight without trouble."

How come no one ever gave him good news? "And how long will that take?"

"No idea. But don't worry, Lord Shenk will find the source and deactivate it."

"He's certain to succeed with Lady White's help," Jet added.

The two women glared at each other prompting Axel to look away. It wasn't enough that the ghouls wanted to kill them, he had those two behind him looking like they wanted to kill each other. This was why he was glad there were no women in the army. They made things too complicated.

A deafening roar came from the gathered ghouls and as one they charged.

The instant they passed into the portal's light they slowed. But they didn't stop. At a steady run, their skin burning and flaking off, howling like the damned, they came on.

Axel met the first ghoul with an overhead chop that took its head and right arm off.

The creature had barely collapsed when another took its place.

He hacked and slashed, cutting down anything not in a uniform.

One of the ghouls slipped inside his guard.

Before it could chomp down on him, a blast of lightning drove it back enough for him to run it through. Corina might not be his brother, but Axel was reminded once again how nice it was to have a wizard on his side.

As quick as it began, the attack ended. The ghouls pulled back out of the light, leaving about two score of their fellows behind.

"Anyone hurt?" Axel asked.

The silence indicated his people had weathered the first attack without casualties. So far so good.

———

Otto followed Lady White down a hall so narrow his shoulders almost brushed the walls. In the feeble light of his spell, the walls and floor appeared made of the same black stone and tile as the passages of the main pyramid. Corruption filled the air and it took all his self-control not to throw up.

Resting his hand on the hilt of his mithril sword helped a little, but he really wanted to draw the weapon and burn the corruption away. That, unfortunately, would foul up whatever magic Lady White was using to track the source of the corruption. Not that the task could be that hard given that the hall hadn't branched yet.

After a minute of walking as quickly as they dared, Otto asked, "Is it me or are we going down?"

"It's not you. The angle has been getting steeper by the moment. We're getting closer to the source of the corruption."

She sounded happy about that. As an undead creature, this sort of environment was probably invigorating for her. He shuddered and kept his opinions to himself. Axel must have engaged the ghouls by now. They needed to hurry and shut off the flow of corruption.

"Do you have any better sense of the source?" he asked.

"It's demonic, but I can't tell much more. It feels different from Astaroth's power. In fact it feels like no flavor of infernal magic I know. Granted my knowledge is limited given how much the other cults hide. Still, this is bizarre. I'm eager to find out what the Arcane Lord has done."

Ordinarily Otto would have been right there with her, but right now all he cared about was how to shut it down. Time was not on their side. If he had to cut the magic apart, he'd do it without a second thought.

The slope continued to deepen until they reached an actual set of stairs.

"It's not far now," Lady White said. "Unless I miss my guess, we're no longer under the pyramid but rather somewhere between them. Though it pains me, this is a good time to draw that sword of yours."

Otto didn't need to be told twice. He pulled the blade and immediately some of the oppressive weight vanished.

She set out again and he followed, careful of his footing, trying his best to watch for traps that would no doubt be invisible to the naked eye anyway. Otto hadn't been this tense in a long time. Something told him that whatever they found, it wouldn't be pleasant.

They reached the bottom of the stairs without issue and found themselves at the entrance to a high, domed cavern. In the center of the chamber, a magic circle crackled with black lightning. In the center of the circle, a creature out of nightmare writhed and thrashed, trying to break free and getting zapped for its trouble.

The demon, for it could be nothing else, resembled a blot of darkness with random mouths and eyes forming and getting absorbed so fast he barely had time to register them. Despite its mouths appearing and vanishing at a rapid clip, it still managed to issue a mind-numbing moan that Otto feared would make his ears bleed. He'd take the pounding of the hammers in Garen any day.

Black energy rose off the creature and was drawn left and right through the walls and out of sight. Otto didn't bother trying to trace it. He had a pretty good idea where it was going.

Lady White stared at the creature with a rapt expression.

"What is it?" he asked.

She gave a little shake as whatever spell she was under broke. "It's an Amalgam of Souls. I've only heard about them. I suppose it's only natural that an Arcane Lord would have been the person to actually create one."

"Okay, what is it and how do we kill it?"

"Basically, Amet Sur caught the souls of the dying before they transformed into energy and were absorbed into heaven or hell. One by one he squashed them together and bound them to the mortal realm. I assume that's what the circle does. The black lightning is torturing them to generate corruption which is what's messing with the portal. The smaller pyramids likely serve as control and focusing units. It must have taken decades at least to accomplish all this."

"Sounds about right for an Arcane Lord. How do we stop it?"

When she didn't answer right away Otto's throat tightened. Time was not on their side here.

At last she said, "We need to set it free. That will end the flow of corruption."

"Great, how do we do that?"

"There's a catch."

He scrubbed a hand across his face. Wasn't there always? "Such as?"

"Once it's free, it will almost certainly try and kill us. I can't begin to guess how to control such a thing. So you're going to have to carve it apart one soul at a time. I can protect you from its aura of corruption, but not for long."

That didn't sound good to Otto, especially given that they had no idea how many souls Amet Sur had used to create the creature. On the other hand, the longer they waited the better the odds that Axel and the others were torn apart. He refused to allow that. Not to mention that, most amazing of all, at least to him, he'd actually come to like his brother for the first time maybe ever.

"How do I free it?"

"That part at least is simple. Take your mithril blade and make a cut across the circle. Once the binding is broken, so is the spell."

Otto drew his sword and took a step toward the circle.

Lady White caught him by the shoulder. "If you get too close, the corruption will reduce you to nothing in an instant. You need to create an ethereal construct to hold the sword."

Otto grimaced. The corruption would burn away pure ether as quickly as flesh, assuming he could even gather enough to build a construct. As he stared at his sword the answer came to him. He'd use the mithril to purify the ether before he built the tentacle. As long as he kept the flow passing through his sword, it should work.

But there was only way to find out for sure.

Drawing ether from around the blade, he pulled it into the metal then back out, creating a slowly expanding sphere of useable energy. The process took far longer than he would have preferred, but at last he had enough to do what he needed.

The tentacle formed at his command and he released the sword. Like a drill through wood, the mithril blade bored its way through the corruption.

Every foot cost Otto energy as he replaced what the corruption burned away. Sweat poured down his face and his whole body trembled.

With two feet to go his knees started to wobble.

Come on!

With a final effort he slashed across the circle, breaking the binding spell. At once the black lightning vanished. The oppressive air filling the room only grew deeper as the Amalgam of Souls rose toward the ceiling.

Somehow Otto didn't fall, but his whole body ached. Lady White was at his side in an instant. She put her arm around him, offering support.

"That was impressive," she said.

"Thanks."

"Pity the hard part is yet to come."

He swallowed a sigh. Somehow he knew she was going to say that.

A xel hacked down another ghoul. The beasts had made a third charge and this one was the strongest so far. It felt like they grew more powerful by the second while Axel's sword felt heavier with every swing. No matter how many they killed, it seemed like more showed up to replace them. Whatever magic summoned the creatures must have called every ghoul in the desert.

Not a terribly encouraging thought.

He had no doubt that the mithril weapons were the only thing keeping them in this fight. He risked a glance left and right. He had two wounded men behind the line, but so far, no fatalities. Heaven had to be watching over them. Nothing else could explain that kind of luck.

A snarling ghoul leapt at him, jaws snapping and saliva flying.

Axel bashed it in the head with his pommel and chopped its head off.

Sweat stung his eyes and he swiped his sleeve across them. On his right, Hans was hard pressed by a pair of ghouls.

Axel hacked one of their arms off and the distraction gave Hans the space he needed to run the second one through.

The rest of the ghouls pulled back a dozen yards to let their numbers replenish for another charge. Axel didn't believe for a moment that they'd give up, no matter how many the scouts killed. They seemed to give no thought to what passed for their lives.

"We can't keep this up much longer." Hans panted for air. "When do we risk the portal?"

"We don't," Corina said from behind them. "The corruption's getting worse by the moment. Anyone using it will be dead instantly. Trust in my master. He'll come through."

Axel had great confidence in his brother, it was the timeline he worried about. Otto couldn't know how hard pressed they were. It would be cold comfort to have the portal cleansed only for them all to be dead.

"Here they come," Cobb said, cutting the debate short.

Axel took a two-handed grip on his sword and hacked down the first ghoul to move into range. At this point he could hardly swing the weapon with one hand. Any sort of skill had given way to brute force and determination. Against a human opponent, they'd have been killed long ago. But the undead seemed to have no understanding of tactics beyond charge in and try to overwhelm them with ferocity.

In their defense, it might actually work this time.

One of the scouts went down on a ghoul's claws.

Axel rushed over and cut the creature's head off.

Too late.

His scout's throat had been ripped open.

Fury drove Axel to new efforts.

He hacked and slashed, cutting down anything that got close.

The ghouls started to pull back. They hissed and raised their hands.

Had he finally frightened them? That seemed unlikely at this point. A moment later one of them started to smoke. It howled and burst into flame.

Axel looked back at Corina, expecting magic.

She grinned. "He did it! The flow of corruption has stopped. The portal is repairing itself and the pure ether is burning them."

She'd barely finished speaking when two more burst into flames. Like a signal, all the ghouls turned and fled out of sight. In seconds they were alone again.

Axel fell to his knees, his sword falling from numb fingers. They'd survived. Most of them anyway.

"Cobb. Take the wounded through the portal and to a healer." He turned to Corina. "It's safe now, right?"

"I'd give it five more minutes just to be sure, but it's pretty close," she said.

"You heard the lady. The rest of us will wait for my brother."

While Cobb organized the injured, Hans plopped to the ground beside Axel. "That was too close. I'm sorry about your man."

"Thanks. Honestly, it's a wonder we only lost one. How are your men?"

"Tired, but intact. I'll take that. When we get back, I'll buy you drink at the Thirsty Sprite. Heaven knows we've earned one."

"I'd say we've earned several." Axel held out his hand and Hans shook it.

CHAPTER 23

T he Amalgam of Souls floated near the ceiling, some of its faces staring upward and others wailing and gnashing their teeth. It still oozed corruption, but not in the volume it did while trapped in the circle. After Lady White's warning, he'd expected it to attack them immediately. Instead, it seemed more lost and forlorn than aggressive.

Three faces formed, each distinct and human, two women and a man. They stared at Otto, expressions pleading without words. There was no anger in them, only pain and anguish. How could anyone make such a thing?

Otto had killed to power the enchanted crystals and to save Wolfric. And if he had to, he would do it again without hesitation. But to create something like this was madness. Whatever remained of Amet Sur's humanity was clearly long gone. Valtan had been right about that at least. The world was certainly better off without Amet Sur.

Still, he didn't know how to help the vile creature. Anything he did might be considered an attack and draw a retaliation. Much as he hated to leave it like this, right now he didn't have the time to figure anything else out.

He turned toward the exit and glanced at Lady White. "Let's go."

"You're just going to leave it there?"

"It doesn't seem interested in a fight. And I'm not at all sure about the right move. Frankly I figured it would be more aggressive considering your warning."

"Everything I've read, and that's little enough, says they should be insane forces of destruction attacking everything they encounter. This one is just kind of pathetic."

"You said they were made up of souls captured at the moment of death. Maybe this one just wants to go on to whatever fate awaits it."

Natural curiosity piqued, Otto walked back toward the amalgam. Holding his hands out to the side to show he wasn't armed, he said, "Can you understand me?"

Five new faces formed in its body and they all stared at Otto. When it spoke, it was an ear-bruising chorus of disharmonic voices. "Free! Free! Free! Us! Us!"

So he was right. Corina and the others were waiting but he couldn't leave this thing here. Heaven knew what mischief someone like Jackal or Ginevera might get up to if they found it. And setting it free would be a kindness.

"How are they made exactly?" Otto asked.

"Exactly? I'm not sure. Up until now, they were more theoretical than practical. Looks like they're stitched together with threads of corruption. Cut the threads and it should fall apart into its constituent parts."

If there was one thing mithril was good for, it was cutting corruption.

Otto slowly drew his sword, charged it with ether, and sent it flying up to the amalgam. More faces appeared in its flesh. They stared at the sword like it was a divine revelation.

Before he could speak again, the creature rushed his sword.

An explosion of corruption rushed out like air out of a burst balloon.

Otto's skin burned and his throat closed up. He couldn't breathe. His eyes felt like they might burst.

A moment later the pain faded as a dark dome appeared around them. Lady White stood over him and shook her head. "That was imprudent."

Otto coughed and spat until his throat worked again. "It seemed like a good idea in the moment. The creature, at least, has returned to where it belongs. We need to do the same."

"Easy for you to say. You can travel by portal. What am I supposed to do?"

"Head northwest until you see the city then retreat east until you find a beach. I'll send a ship for you as soon as I can. I doubt the undead will bother you once we're gone."

"I suppose that will work. Lord of the Dead isn't likely to send another hunter, at least not right away. Jackal's loss will weaken his position with the other lords. With any luck, he might not even survive."

Otto stood and found his legs reasonably steady. "What are the odds of that?"

"Slim, but a girl can hope."

Otto grinned. "Can this barrier move with us? I need to collect my sword before we leave."

"No problem. The corruption is already dissipating. Ten more minutes and we won't need it at all."

Otto had wasted all the time he cared to and as soon as they found his sword, they headed for the exit. The moment they stepped outside he took a deep breath. Who would have thought that the air of the Dead Lands could ever taste fresh? After that cursed chamber, he suspected anything short of an abattoir would have been an improvement.

Lady White held back as he headed for the portal. "I'll set out now. Take Jet back with you. She'd just slow me down."

"Will do. And thanks for your help. This wouldn't have gone nearly so well without you."

Even knowing what she was, he couldn't help being struck by the beauty of her smile. "Do you know, this might be the first time anyone's thanked me for my efforts?"

"I suppose manners aren't a priority for demon worshippers. When you make it to the empire, I'm looking forward to many long, pleasant conversations. Safe journey."

She waved and started out into the city. Amazing what simple kindness got you. Even the undead needed a word of appreciation now and then. He touched the gold and mithril medallion under his tunic. Willing cooperation was so much more valuable than coercion.

Otto hurried on to the portal where he found Axel and the others waiting a few feet from the entrance. At a glance, Otto saw that the corruption had nearly been purified. Excellent, they could head home in moments.

"You cut it close enough." Axel came over and shook his hand. "Two more minutes and we'd have had it."

"I see you lost one man." Otto nodded toward the wrapped body. "What happened?"

"A ghoul broke through his guard. He was dead before I reached his side."

"I'm sorry, but we'll have to burn the body." Axel's expression twisted like it did when Otto told him he'd killed the plague bearers in Straken. "I don't say this lightly. Anyone killed by a ghoul will rise as one in twenty-four hours. He either needs to be burned or beheaded. As his commanding officer, I leave the decision in your hands. I also need his sword if it's handy."

He'd barely finished talking when Corina came running over, a sullen Jet right behind. "I knew you'd make it in time. What happened?"

"The same thing that always happens. Some nasty monster had to be destroyed. I'll tell you about it once matters are settled." Otto turned his attention to Jet. "Lady White has gone north toward the coast. She said you're to come back with us. I'll be sending a ship to retrieve her as soon as we reach Lux."

Jet blew out a sigh. "Abandoned again. She really thinks little of me."

"Not at all," Otto said. "But as you are now, you're more of a liability than a help. Once you learn a bit of magic, that will change. Just ask Corina. She was once where you are now."

There was a wet whack and Otto turned to see Axel standing over the now headless body of his scout. It would have been a kindness to everyone had he simply let Otto burn the body, but it was Axel's call.

He glanced at the portal again. Not a speck of darkness remained. "We're good to go. Everyone through the portal."

Otto waited until the last scout passed through then followed. There was a moment where the ether streaked past him then he stepped out into the Garen fort. The wounded were already being loaded into wagons for the ride to Branik's temple. The healers there would fix them up in a day or two.

"What now, my lord?" Hans asked.

"Now we go to Lux and send every ship we can find out

searching for Eddred." Otto turned to Gareth. "But first, this gentleman and I have some business to conclude."

Gareth eagerly held out his arm. Otto sent fine threads of ether into the mithril bracelet. The magic was simple enough. Basically it worked like one of his rune coins. Half a minute's work drew all the ether out of the bracelet. Once that was done, Otto pulled with a pair of ten-thread tentacles.

The bracelet expanded and slipped off Gareth's arm. Otto held it out to him. "Want to keep it as a souvenir? I've negated the magic that allowed you to be tracked."

"No, I'd just as soon never lay eyes on it again." Gareth pulled the sheathed dagger off his belt. "You said something about a mithril sword."

"Indeed, I did. Hans, fetch the dead scout's weapon."

Hans did as he was told and held out the weapon to Gareth. The exchange was made and Gareth couldn't stop staring at the weapon in his hands. It was probably the most valuable thing he'd ever owned. At least in his mind. His dagger was actually far more valuable, but Otto didn't plan to mention that.

"What are your intentions now?" Otto asked.

"You mentioned sending a ship to collect Lady White," Gareth said. "Any chance I could catch a ride to the City of Coins? I'd like to try my luck there."

"That's fine. We'll be heading to Lux shortly. I'll have the captain drop you off before picking up Lady White."

"Can I go too?" Jet asked. "I'd like to catch up with her as soon as possible."

Otto wasn't certain what Lady White would think about that, but he was happy to be rid of Jet. "Certainly. One more passenger isn't going to matter."

Otto's stomach growled and he yawned. He really needed a

hot meal and sleep. Even if Eddred was already on his way home, it would take at least a week for him to reach Markane. They had plenty of time. Yet everything in Otto screamed to get the ships out and a search pattern working now.

Given how his mission had gone so far, he refused to take any chances.

CHAPTER 24

Eddred's sleep had been marred by nightmares ever since returning to his ship. Every time he closed his eyes, he saw Adam and Lilly's dead bodies lying on the floor of the pyramid. He'd abandoned them and couldn't let it go. He didn't want to let it go. Their deaths were just one more reminder of everything that had gone wrong since that fateful day at the Conclave.

If only he had the strength to stand up to the other kings. He could have stopped all this before it happened. But he'd stayed silent and followed Valtan's lead, just as he always did, and now thousands were dead. If he never enjoyed another sound night's sleep, it would be a just punishment. He dearly hoped Otto Shenk suffered as many sleepless nights as he did.

Somehow he doubted the young wizard suffered from the same doubts. No one could do what he'd done if they suffered from any sort of conscience.

He finally rolled out of his narrow bed and got dressed. The Scroll sat on top of his strongbox. It seemed to cast a shadow far too big for its size. That was Eddred's imagination of course. It was just a rolled-up piece of parchment, whatever its secrets.

Eddred tied his boots and took a step for the door. Immediately he turned back and picked up the Scroll. He couldn't leave it lying there where anyone might pick it up. Not that anyone was apt to. He trusted his crew absolutely and a scroll made of human flesh wasn't the sort of thing a thief would grab.

Up on deck, the wind blew his hair and the salty mist hit his face. The sails snapped overhead as the wind gusted. He blew out a sigh and looked over the water. The sea still soothed him, at least a little bit. They were only a couple days out from Lordes. On his right, towering cliffs protected the island from invasion. Soon he'd be free to dump his problems at Valtan's feet and return to the little village he'd called home before this most recent misadventure.

At the helm, Captain Carter kept a tight grip on the wheel. They'd been at full sail virtually nonstop for days. That nothing had happened was a testament to both the captain and crew.

Captain Carter nodded at Eddred's approach. "Majesty. Did you sleep?"

"Some. How much further?"

"Two days, give or take. We'd have been there by now if we'd set a direct course." There was no rebuke in Carter's tone, just a statement of fact.

"The wolves will be watching the direct route," Eddred said. "My hope is that by coming in wide and making a loop to the north, we'll sneak in behind them."

They'd had the debate a handful of times already, but it made Eddred feel better to say it again out loud. Like if he kept repeating it, he'd make the theory a reality.

He shivered, and not from the northern chill.

A moment later a voice from above rang out. "Sail off the starboard bow!"

Eddred ran to the front of the ship and stared out over the water. Please let it be a fisherman.

Even at a distance he could tell there was too much sail out for a trawler. No merchants traveled this way, not on business. It had to be a search vessel. If Otto had deployed ships this far northeast, he must have requisitioned every ship in Lux. As long as it didn't have any war wizards aboard, they should be okay.

"She's changing course!" the lookout called. "Moving to cut us off."

Eddred ran back to the helm. "Can we outmaneuver them?"

"Probably." Captain Carter looked up at the crow's nest. "Can you make out what kind of ship it is?"

"A two-masted trader. No weapons I can see."

"Unless they plan to ram us, there's no way they can stop this ship."

Reassured by the captain's confidence, Eddred relaxed a fraction. This lasted just long enough for the lookout to shout, "She's turning hard southwest."

"They're running to warn the rest of the hunters." Eddred wanted to punch something. "There'll be a dozen ships between us and the harbor. All of them armed and manned by wizards. May they all burn in whatever hell awaits them!"

"There's another option," Captain Carter said. "There's a small inlet about twenty miles from here. We can put you ashore there. While the ships wait for us, you can sneak off to the city."

Eddred shook his head. The curse that killed everything on the main island would finish him off before he took ten steps.

But there was another option. Valtan had proven he could appear as far as the barrier islands in spirit form.

"Make for West Barrier Island. Hopefully Lord Valtan will sense our arrival and meet us there before anyone that wants to sink us shows up."

"Yes, Majesty." Captain Carter adjusted their course a few points west.

Eddred really hoped he was right about this. Getting so close to the end only to fail now would break him.

And the world.

———

By some miracle, Eddred reached West Barrier Island without interference near sunset. A short pier jutted out into the ocean, too short to accommodate their ship. His luck had been so rotten, any moment now Eddred expected to see a Garenland ship rushing up to sink them. Happily, the ocean remained free of sails.

In the rigging, sailors rushed to take down sails as Captain Carter brought them around to anchor. Even though he knew the men were doing their absolute best, Eddred couldn't shake the feeling that every second was a second they couldn't spare.

At last the anchor clattered over the side and splashed into the water. He didn't even wait for it to set before ordering a rowing party into the dinghy. The men appreciated his desire for haste and they were pulling for shore in record time.

Eddred clutched the Scroll in his fist. Please, please let Valtan sense their arrival.

On shore, at the end of the dock, a handful of villagers stood waiting to greet them. He tried to remember if he'd ever actually visited the island before. He must have. When he inherited the crown, he made a full tour of the kingdom. He was equally sure he hadn't been back since. That was a bit embarrassing really, but no one ever came to court to complain.

When he reached the end of the dock, an older man with a white beard and wearing homespun brown trousers and a frayed tunic bowed. He had to be the leader of the nearby village. "Welcome, Majesty. What brings you to our small island?"

"Nothing good I'm afraid. I was hoping—"

The ether crackled to his left and a moment later an image of Valtan appeared. "You have it?"

Eddred held out the Scroll and waved it at him like it was a sword. "They all died to get this. Adam, Lilly, and Uther, they're all dead. I hope it was worth the price."

Valtan hung his head, suddenly seeming all of his thousands of years old. "To keep this out of Otto Shenk's hands is worth any price. But I would not have seen those three die. That it was for a good cause is small comfort, but I do hope you take some."

"The only comfort I want is for you to take this cursed scroll as far away from me as possible. Do that, and I will be happy never to see you again."

Valtan's face twisted like Eddred had stabbed him. "Everything I've done has been for the greater good. I gave up everything to protect you mortals, both from my former friends and from yourselves. Am I truly so deserving of your disdain?"

"I have no strength left to care." Eddred made a dismissive wave. "Take your prize and leave me in peace. I've done all I plan to do for you."

Valtan's expression fell. Whatever response he'd hoped for, Eddred hadn't given it to him. "So be it. Good luck to you."

Valtan's form dissolved into a pool of light that dragged the Scroll back toward Lordes out of sight. Eddred mustered some satisfaction from that. Lilly and Adam hadn't died for nothing. He'd very much like to see Otto try and claim the Scroll now. If the curse didn't kill him, Valtan certainly would.

"Back to the ship, everyone," he said. "Our work here is finished."

"Will you not at least stay for the evening meal?" the chief asked. "It will be ready soon. While I admit it's not much, it would surely be better than ship's rations."

"Thank you for your generosity." Eddred felt moved nearly to tears by the offer. How long had it been since someone offered him simple kindness without wanting something in return? Not since South Barrier Island. "Unfortunately we need to leave."

Eddred held out his hand and the village chief seemed to debate which would be a bigger insult, touching his king or refusing the handshake. At last a calloused hand wrapped around Eddred's and gave it an enthusiastic pump.

"Even this short visit was an honor for us, Majesty."

Eddred smiled. At least he'd made one person happy. He led the sailors back to the dinghy and they rowed back to the ship.

Captain Carter met him at the rail and pulled him aboard. "Orders, Majesty?"

"Set sail, make for the capital."

"Are we not likely to encounter a number of enemies there?"

"I guarantee it."

"Then, perhaps it would be best to flee? We have more than enough supplies to make it back to the City of Coins."

"I'm done running. Besides, when that ship reports our location, someone will come here looking. Even if they don't find us, they will find the village. Nothing our enemies have done makes me think they'll be gentle with their questions. If you want to leave behind all but the minimum crew, I'll allow it."

Captain Carter drew himself up. "We've been by your side since the beginning of this mess, Majesty. We'll be there at the end as well."

The crew all gave enthusiastic shouts of agreement.

Eddred had expected no less, but he wanted to make sure everyone knew that he wouldn't think less of anyone that wanted to remain behind. "Thank you all for your loyalty. When you're ready, Captain, take us home."

CHAPTER 25

Otto paced on the deck of the *Sea Star.* The sky was a stunning blue and so clear he could see the moon. Under different circumstances, this might have been a pleasant trip. But he was in no mood to relax. If Captain Wainwright had any complaints about his endless meandering, he was wise enough to keep them to himself.

They'd been patrolling the waters near Lordes' harbor for over a week, being careful not to sail into Valtan's range. Eddred's ship had to be getting close. In fact, he should have been here before now.

A day ago, one of the scout ships returned to report that Eddred's ship had been spotted to the northwest. That was both good news and bad since the ship that located him didn't have weapons or a war wizard on board. They'd been forced to return at best speed to report.

As soon as word reached him, Otto had dispatched a pair of heavily armed interceptors to capture the king. He expected to hear word of their success soon. And the waiting was driving him mad. He was so close to ultimate success he could taste it.

The miserable pest Eddred had done everything in his power to keep Otto from his destiny. When he finally realized his complete failure, the man's pain would be sweet indeed.

"Ship approaching!" the lookout cried. "She's flying the flag of Markane!"

That couldn't be right. Was Eddred mad enough to think he could force his way past the blockade? It was only two ships, but given that Otto was on one of them, he had no hope of winning past.

"She's slowing and put up her sails!"

Otto's frown deepened and he extended his sight. Sure enough Eddred stood on deck. He wore a fine silk tunic and crisp white trousers. All the sailors looked dressed in their finest clothes as well. What was he playing at?

Otto gathered his power and said, "Bring us alongside. Someone get Hans and his men up here."

A sailor ran to fetch the good sergeant while Captain Wainwright adjusted his course. Otto moved to the front of the ship, his every sense alert for a trap. Not that they had much hope with both their wizards dead. Frankly they couldn't have done much even if those two weaklings were still alive.

"Lord Shenk?" Hans and the guys stopped behind him, swords buckled on and looking ready for a fight. Pity Eddred didn't seem inclined to give them one.

"Our prey has kindly put in an appearance. As soon as we're alongside, we'll board and claim the Scroll. I don't think Eddred is capable of a trap under these circumstances but keep focused. I don't want to lose anyone else, not when we're so close."

"Understood, my lord," Hans said. "What are we going to do with Eddred?"

"If he comes along quietly, we'll take him to the emperor. Wolfric can decide his fate."

Not that Otto especially cared, but as one of the few kings that betrayed them still living, he figured Wolfric would find some amusement in having him hung or beheaded or whatever. Maybe they could take him to Straken and have him dig mithril beside King Uther. That would be a fitting fate.

After a bit of delicate maneuvering, Captain Wainwright brought them alongside Eddred's ship. Grappling hooks were tossed and soon enough Otto and the others leapt across the gap, swords drawn.

No one tried to stop the boarding party. In fact, everyone visible was unarmed. Eddred stood alone in the center of the deck. Hate filled his eyes when he glared at Otto, but he didn't curse or rage. In fact, the king seemed far too calm given the situation. A dark feeling washed over Otto, but he dismissed it. Whatever was going to happen, would happen regardless.

"Hand over the Scroll," Otto said.

"I already did." Eddred held his hands out to the side as if to show he didn't have it and smiled. "Valtan has it now."

"Impossible. No one has entered the harbor."

"We didn't have to. Valtan's range extends to the east, west, and south barrier islands. It takes all his power, but he can extend his awareness and even bring items back to the capital with him. Small items, but then, the Scroll isn't terribly heavy. Best of luck trying to reclaim it."

Eddred wasn't lying, Otto saw that without using magic. No amount of torture could force him to hand over something he didn't have. He didn't even have to compel him to say where he'd hidden it. The problem was, even with all the information he needed in hand, taking the Scroll from the last living

Arcane Lord, even as diminished as Valtan was, would be a nearly impossible task.

Lucky Otto had a dagger that could stop magic.

"Orders, my lord?" Hans asked.

"Clap Eddred in irons and bring him to our ship." Otto turned to the crew. "You will follow us to Lux and tie up at the dock. Do anything else, and you can watch me chop pieces off your king until you comply."

One of Hans's men bound Eddred's hands behind his back with iron manacles and Otto led them over to the *Sea Star*. Eddred offered no resistance and in fact seemed perfectly content with his situation. Clearly his mind had broken at some point on his voyage home.

Otto was just glad to have the fool out of his way. Ineffectual though he was, Eddred had managed to cause him more than a few delays. There was more than a little irony in the fact that the weakest of the kings lasted the longest and did the most harm.

"You'll never get it now," Eddred said. "I don't care how strong you are, Valtan will crush you like a bug if you challenge him."

"Maybe," Otto said. "But I doubt you'll be around to find out."

CHAPTER 26

Valtan sat in his workshop surrounded by a collection of magic and knowledge beyond the conception of a mortal wizard. He knew why he'd chosen this place to begin his work. Not the reason he told himself, that he might need some esoteric reference or magical device, but the real reason. Being surrounded by these things helped him remember that he was the last Arcane Lord, not the scared young man he'd been when he first met Amet Sur.

The rolled-up scroll resting peacefully on the pale marble surface of the bench in front of him reeked of Amet's magic. It reminded him too much of the curse that destroyed his city. That it was made of human skin did nothing to help his nerves.

He'd been staring at the blasted thing for two days.

Two days!

But today was the day. He'd worked up his courage, drank a bottle of port even though he couldn't get drunk, and done everything else he could think of to build up his courage.

Valtan laughed at himself. If only Eddred could see him

now, terrified and indecisive. A far cry from the image he projected any time he was around others.

To hell with it!

He snatched up the Scroll and before he could think better of it unrolled the yellowed parchment. It measured about three feet long. Amet's precise writing covered every inch from top to bottom. Valtan had heard of the Scroll of course, they all had. It was supposed to contain his greatest secrets, including how to use the Immortality Engine to transform a wizard that had overcome their personal limit into an Arcane Lord.

As he read, it became increasingly clear that this scroll held nothing of the sort. Instead of magical secrets, it held a detailed biography of Amet's life, from birth until the moment of Valtan's betrayal. All the major moments were there along with others that would have been important only to him.

When he finished reading, he tossed the Scroll back on his workbench. Valtan wanted to strangle Eddred. The idiot had clearly found a false scroll and, believing it genuine, brought it back.

He turned and started pacing. No, he shouldn't be so harsh. The scroll was powerfully enchanted. Anyone would believe it was genuine and only a fool would try to read it without precautions. As expected, Amet really had hidden his greatest treasure well. The real problem was that if the actual Sanguine Scroll was still out there, Otto Shenk might yet find it. Even worse, Valtan had no more agents to send on a recovery mission.

What was he supposed to do?

As he pondered his options, a question popped into his head. How had Amet recorded the betrayal when he couldn't have known about it beforehand?

A surge of ethereal corruption filled the workshop.

Valtan spun and found the Scroll floating above his desk, black lightning coursing through and around it. He raised a shield just in time.

The first blast struck him, shattering his shield, and knocking him backward. How did he store so much power in the Scroll? It wasn't possible. All evidence to the contrary.

He screamed when the next blast struck his chest, incinerating his tunic and sending him sprawling. He hadn't felt pain like this in a thousand years. Even activating the portals off schedule felt like a tickle in comparison.

Valtan tried to become one with the ether, but there was too much corruption around him.

He pushed himself to a sitting position just in time for the Scroll to slap into his chest. A moment later he screamed as it began fusing to his chest. Small tendrils dug into his skin and dragged the scroll in every direction.

It expanded, quickly covering his lower torso and moving toward his shoulders.

Gathering his wits and power, Valtan shaped the ether into a blade. Steeling himself, he tried to cut the parchment off.

Any damage he did repaired itself instantly. The Scroll was as connected to the ether as he was.

In desperation he formed a bubble around himself, cutting off its link.

The expansion stopped, thank heaven. Now he needed to find a way to undo the damage.

You can't undo it.

Amet Sur's voice echoed in his mind, as dark, rich, and evil as he remembered.

"A simulacrum."

Far more than that, old friend. Did you imagine I would be so easy to get rid of? I was ancient five thousand years before you were born. Your betrayal hurt, I admit that, but unlike the others, I was prepared. I had intended to use the overly ambitious boy's body for my return, but then your pawn touched my scroll and I saw in his mind how weakened you were. The thought of claiming your body as my own was too delicious.

"The Scroll is your phylactery. In the instant before your body was destroyed, you shifted your soul back to it." If that was right, Valtan was in serious trouble. Even at full strength, he had never been a match for Amet. Neither of them was at their best, but he still doubted he could win.

I always said you were my brightest disciple. And you're quite correct. While I had no intention of sitting in my pyramid for centuries, everything else is working as I intended. Now, be a good fellow, bring down this barrier, and let me finish my rebirth.

"I didn't save this world just to hand it to a butcher like you. The mortals have built their own world without us and despite their many flaws, it's a good thing. Better than what we made." Valtan settled onto the floor and entered a meditative trance. He could keep the barrier up indefinitely this way.

Be reasonable. You're only delaying the inevitable. Whether it takes a week or a century, your focus will eventually slip. And when it does, your body will be mine.

Valtan grit his teeth. We'll see about that.

CHAPTER 27

When Otto delivered Eddred to Wolfric, he'd been surprised by his friend's lack of excitement. He'd simply ordered the former king taken away and put in the dungeon. Now the two of them were alone in the throne room, even Commander Borden had been dismissed.

Wolfric climbed down from his throne and walked to Otto's side. He placed a hand on his shoulder and asked, "What's troubling you, my friend?"

Otto had thought he'd kept his emotions pretty well hidden, but it seemed he'd failed. Either that or Wolfric had become more perceptive while he was gone.

"I failed. Valtan has the Scroll. Now I have to figure out how to defeat an Arcane Lord in order to become one. Appropriate I suppose, but I had hoped to delay the final confrontation until I could face him as an equal."

"You might not be an Arcane Lord, but you're the cleverest man I know. If anyone can figure out how to do the impossible, it's you. After all, you've already done it several times. Why not take all the war wizards and simply overwhelm him?"

"Won't work. The curse that destroyed Lordes will kill anyone that sets foot on the island and I only have one ring that offers protection from the spell. Whatever happens, I'll be facing him alone."

"Is there nothing you can do to even the odds?" Wolfric asked.

"There is, but it will be an inconvenience for the empire."

Wolfric waved off his concern. "The empire can never repay you for everything you've done. Whatever you require shall be done. Should anyone complain, send them to me and I'll have their heads removed."

"In that case, I'm going to activate all the portals at once. With all of them pulling power from Valtan, it should put us on even footing, powerwise. There's nothing I can do about the difference in experience."

"Surely a couple thousand years couldn't make that much difference."

Otto stared at Wolfric for a moment then threw his head back and laughed. He laughed until his ribs ached and his doubts were gone. Maybe he couldn't win and maybe he could, but either way he meant to give it everything he had. He would either succeed or die trying. He'd come too far to just give up.

He wiped the tears from his eyes. "Thank you for that. I can't remember the last time I laughed."

"Happy to be of help. Now, an order from your emperor. Go home, rest, eat, play with your daughter. Only when you have recovered all your strength do you have my permission to undertake this impossible task."

Otto nodded. While he had no desire to see his family, the resting and recovering was a good idea. If he was at anything less than his best when he faced Valtan, he'd be dead before the battle even started.

"Wise council. Why don't you stop by and join us for dinner tonight?" Otto didn't mention that having Wolfric there to distract Annamaria would make the night pass quicker for everyone.

"I'll take you up on that offer. I've come to think of Abby as something of a niece. An evening of play and conversation would be just the thing. Say seven?"

"I'll let everyone know. It's good to be home." That was the first completely true thing Otto had said and he meant it from the bottom of his heart.

———

Otto and Corina walked side by side through the afternoon streets of Gold Ward with Hans and the guys a few steps behind. It felt like the first time they'd relaxed in a long time. Not that Otto was really relaxed, not with the upcoming confrontation with Valtan on his mind, but at least he didn't expect an attack to come out of nowhere.

That was a nice change of pace.

They weren't the only ones out enjoying the nice afternoon weather. The streets were remarkably busy for Gold Ward. Usually the rich and powerful took carriages, but today they all seemed eager for the fresh air. Everyone gave him looks of respect or a nod of greeting, but no one approached to talk. That was fine with Otto, his tolerance for foolish chitchat was low at the best of times.

"Did the emperor really just lock Eddred up?" Corina asked. "I figured he'd have hung him right away."

"As did I. Maybe having him locked up is enough for Wolfric. He's mellowed a lot since the assassins, more than I expected."

"Is that a good thing or a bad thing?" she asked.

"Too soon to tell, but I'm going to say good. A cool head tends to lead to better decisions. Will you be joining us for dinner? As my apprentice, you're practically part of the family, such as it is."

She beamed at the compliment then shook her head. "I'll pass. Your wife doesn't seem to like me. I see her giving me looks when I visit. Do you think she thinks you're having an affair with me?"

Otto swallowed a laugh. He didn't want to hurt Corina's feelings, but given his options, she wasn't near the top of the list of people he'd have an affair with. Besides, Annamaria was hardly in a position to be jealous.

"I doubt it. She just doesn't really know you. Wizards make people nervous. After Abby was kidnapped, she's probably just on edge. Tell you what, if you're not coming, why don't you go check in with Allen and Sin. You can give me a report in the morning."

She brightened at the prospect of a mission. "Count on me."

He was surprised to find that he did. She'd become quite valuable to him. Having a trusted agent, someone that didn't serve out of fear, was tremendously helpful. Other than Corina, he only really trusted Axel, Hans, and Draken. Wolfric too, but he was a noble and, friend or not, Otto knew enough nobles that he would never fully trust one.

They reached the gates of Shenk Manor and the guards hastened to bow and open the iron gates for him.

"Take Hans with you. I expect no trouble, but better safe than sorry." He glanced at Hans who nodded. That one look was enough for him to understand that it was now his job to look after Corina. "We'll meet up at the warehouse tomorrow around midmorning."

Everyone saluted and they parted ways. Otto stared up the path at the manor then turned back. "The emperor is coming to dinner tonight. I wanted to warn you so his arrival wouldn't take you by surprise."

The guards both stiffened. Wolfric's pending arrival would make anyone, but especially a commoner, nervous.

He continued up to the manor and slipped through the front door. The elaborate foyer was empty and the house quiet. Not surprising given the time of day. No doubt everyone was working on something or other. He hadn't been home this early in a long time, so certainly no one would expect him.

Otto hung his cloak on a handy peg and made his way into the dining room. As always, a servant was at her post in case anyone wanted anything from the kitchen. She looked at Otto with nervous brown eyes and smoothed the front of her black and white uniform.

"The emperor will be joining us for dinner. Please let the cook know."

Her eyes got even wider and she quickly ran through the connecting door. He planned to add that they didn't need to go crazy, but it wouldn't have done any good. The cook would want to show off as soon as he knew Wolfric was joining them. He shook his head at the foolish preening that obsessed everyone with any rank. Such a waste of energy.

When he reached the foot of the steps a familiar voice said, "This is a surprise. We seldom see you when the sun is still up."

Otto swallowed a sigh and looked up at his darling wife, Abby cradled in her arms. She wore a simple, pale-blue dress and white slippers. No jewelry decorated her smooth skin. She was still beautiful, there was no denying that.

"I had a break from my work." He climbed the stairs and paused a few feet from her. "The emperor suggested I take a little time to rest before getting back to it. He'll be joining us for dinner tonight."

"How nice, he hasn't been by in a month. I'll let the cook know."

"Already done. You can inform Edwyn if you like." Otto turned to go to his room. He needed to get cleaned up and change out of his dirty clothes. A nap wouldn't hurt anything either. All the magic he'd used in the Dead Lands had left him exhausted and the hunt for Eddred hadn't helped.

"Do you have a moment?" Annamaria asked.

Otto turned back and raised an eyebrow. What the hell could she possibly want now?

"I wanted to tell you that I'm not angry anymore. After you saved Abby, I did a lot of thinking and I understand why you did what you did. I don't expect you to forgive me, but maybe we could be friends, eventually. I'll have to tell Abby something about her father when she gets older."

Otto shrugged. By the time the brat was old enough to understand that her father was a pig that seduced other men's wives, he would likely either be an Arcane Lord or dead. And in either case he wasn't apt to care what she said. In fact, he didn't especially care now.

"Tell her whatever you like. Just keep the consequences of her knowing the truth in mind."

Otto stalked off. Sleep would likely be impossible now, but perhaps he could at least clear his mind enough to be civil company when Wolfric arrived.

———

A week of minimal magic use and plenty of rest had restored Otto to his full strength. Lady White and Jet had returned and Otto set them up in a suite in a seldom-used corner of Franken Manor. He'd find something permanent once matters with Valtan were settled, assuming he survived.

At least the empire was at peace, giving him space to relax. Not that he did nothing. Most of his time was spent in the armory reading every book he could find with anything about Valtan. He found little enough. In the end, the answer to his problem was as obvious as it was simple.

He needed to pay his master a visit. Given her hatred for Valtan, she would be eager to tell him anything that might help. In fact, she expected him to kill the Arcane Lord as part of their bargain. But that wasn't supposed to happen until after he made the transformation himself. That way he could face Valtan on even ground.

He set the book he'd been reading down and stood. He'd done everything possible here. A bone ring gleamed on his finger. The item would protect him from the curse he used to destroy Lordes. He'd searched and searched but found no more of them. He considered taking Lady White with him but didn't dare. She'd proven a valuable and trustworthy ally, but if she chose to betray him in the middle of the fight, that would be the end.

It came down to him and that was all there was to it. Somehow that seemed right. Like a final test to prove he was worthy of the power. He shook his head at the ludicrous idea. The only reason he'd ended up in this situation was bad luck. Fate, destiny, or anything similar had nothing to do with it.

Taking a breath to steady himself, Otto became one with the ether.

A moment later he appeared in the hidden tower. Lord Karonin's face filled the mirror. She appeared to have shaken off whatever bad mood had struck her the last couple times he visited. Thank goodness for that. Otto found her hard enough to deal with when she was in a good mood.

He bowed. "Master."

"Have you found the Scroll?"

"Sort of." He filled her in on what happened in the Dead Lands. "Now I have to face Valtan to claim it. I hoped you might have some advice for me."

"You have no hope of defeating an Arcane Lord as you are now. Best forget about it and accept your current situation."

Otto grimaced. That wasn't at all acceptable. "Will you at least listen to my plan? I've been thinking about it for some time."

"Very well. It's not like I have an excess of entertainment options here."

"First, I'm going to activate all the portals I control at once. That should weaken him considerably."

"True, but the pig is still immortal. And even weakened, he's forgotten more about magic than you'll ever know."

"I also have this." Otto drew the black-bladed dagger. He'd been keeping it on him at all times since acquiring it.

"Sheathe it! At once!"

Her shrill scream prompted him to take a step back and quickly slip the blade into its sheath.

Once he had she said in a calmer voice, "Where did you get that?"

"I traded a thief a mithril sword for it. He claimed it had been in his family for some time."

"Was he from Colt's Land?"

Otto cocked his head. "That's right. How did you know?"

"That black metal, it's called anti-mithril, at least that's what we called it. It's from one of the other worlds we visited. The natives had another name, but I can't recall what it was. It was abundant there. They had no wizards and we thought conquering it would be quick. Little did we know this abundant metal negated all magic. All their weapons and armor was made from it. I'm not ashamed to say we fled and never returned. Amet ordered none of the metal to be brought back. It seems Colt's curiosity got the best of him. The fool never could resist a mystery."

"So, a weapon that even an Arcane Lord fears." Otto's respect for the dagger went up a few notches. "Can it kill Valtan?"

"Of course not, he's immortal. But if you can get close enough to use it, the dagger will put him in a coma until someone pulls the blade out."

Not as good as dead, but it would certainly put Valtan out of the way so he could claim the Scroll. Once he became an Arcane Lord himself, they could have a rematch.

"Master, when we first spoke you said killing Valtan was part of the price of your instruction. Is it actually possible to kill him short of tossing him in the netherworld with you?"

"No. My original intention was to teach you how to open the portal to the netherworld so you could do exactly that. Your current power and skill isn't nearly enough so there was no reason to explain the process to you. When the time comes, it will be far easier if you render him unconscious and immobile with the dagger. It's a powerful weapon, but don't be overconfident. Holding it drawn will cut you off from the ether as well."

A truly double-edged weapon. Still, if he couldn't defeat Valtan with magic, what were his options?

"Good luck, Apprentice. If you succeed in this task, you will have proven yourself worthy of the power of an Arcane Lord."

Otto bowed and forced his nerves aside. He would win this fight. There was no other choice.

CHAPTER 28

Time meant nothing to Valtan as he meditated and maintained the barrier around his body. How long had it been since he'd been without his connection to the ether? For now, he felt as blind as a newborn. Not that he was in any danger. Ironically, the curse that killed the city also protected him from enemies showing up unannounced. Any mortal that set foot on the island would be dead in seconds.

Do you plan to sit here forever? It's pointless to try. Even an Arcane Lord can't maintain total focus eternally. The moment you slip, your body will be mine.

He ignored the hate-filled voice of Amet Sur, his former mentor and the mightiest Arcane Lord. Not that he wasn't right. Valtan recognized how precarious his situation was. His only hope was that he'd come up with a plan before his concentration lapsed.

You're grasping at straws. We both know how this ends. Pretending otherwise is pointless and insulting. Just accept your fate so I can get on with the work of rebuilding what you destroyed.

"Accept my fate, like you would, were our positions reversed?"

Amet's amusement flooded though him.

Fair enough. None of us became Arcane Lords because we lacked determination. I've waited seven hundred years for this moment. I can wait a few more weeks. The best part about being immortal is we have all the time in the world.

Valtan would have happily told Amet to keep silent, but he didn't want to give him the satisfaction of knowing his needling was getting on his nerves.

I'm in your mind, old friend. You can hide nothing from me.

So much for thinking up a plan in secret. Not that he'd been having much luck with that. There was only one way to end this, but to do it would take all his focus and power and even then, he had serious doubts that it would succeed.

You can't imagine I'd simply do nothing while you sent us both to the netherworld. I'll control your body long before you can reach the portal. You—

Valtan roared in pain, cutting Amet off mid-rant. Someone had just activated two portals at once. The pain increased a moment later when a third came online. His shield wavered a fraction and Valtan refocused strengthening it with his quickly diminishing power.

He knew what was happening. That fool Shenk was planning to come after him and he wanted Valtan as weak as possible. Sensible, since there was no way he could know about the psychic battle being fought. Unfortunately for Valtan, Otto was playing directly into Amet's hands.

When the fourth portal activated, his vision darkened. Clenching his jaw. Valtan refused to lose consciousness. That would doom him. He had to control the pain and stay focused no matter what.

That boy is certainly determined. I learned a great deal about him when I read your servant's mind. He might make an excellent first apprentice.

"He'd certainly be a good match for you. You're both bloody-minded monsters." Valtan held his barrier together with nothing but grit and a thousand years of practice.

Amet's psychic laugh echoed through Valtan's brain.

So self-righteous. I don't remember holding a dagger to your throat when we conquered the other worlds. You fought beside us, killed with us. We were brothers in blood and magic. Then you suddenly develop a conscience and think you're better than us. You're a murderer, old friend. And nothing you do will ever change that.

"You're right. But unlike you, I've at least tried to right the wrongs I committed. I've dedicated my life to making this world a place where ordinary humans could live without fear of wizards dominating them again. And I refuse to allow you or anyone else to destroy that."

A fifth portal activated and Valtan lost control. His barrier fell and ether flooded into him. Worse, it flooded into the Scroll attached to his chest. It began expanding again.

This time Valtan was ready. Instead of a barrier around his whole body, he built a magical wall between his untouched flesh and the scroll. Amet pushed against it, but the expansion slowed to a crawl. Slowed but didn't stop.

At least he'd bought time.

Valtan stood and ran out of his workshop, down the stairs to the tower exit, and outside. His best speed was now little more than a shuffle, but he did his best to hurry toward the portal. If he reached it before Amet took over, the world would survive.

If he failed, a new dark age would begin.

———

Otto appeared near the docks in Lordes. He'd spent so much time staring at them while he waited to capture Eddred, that he had no trouble making the trip through the ether. He'd half expected to get grabbed by Valtan again and dragged heaven only knew where, but he'd sensed no sign of him in the ether and he appeared without issue.

He glanced around and shuddered. The stench of death filled the air. The city reminded him of the Dead Lands only with less corruption. Black splotches covered the ground, marking where people had been killed by the curse. Otto still didn't fully understand how the magic worked, but it had certainly gotten his point across. Pity Valtan was too stubborn to take a hint. So many lives could have been spared if he'd just minded his own business.

As the most powerful wizard in the world, he probably thought everything was his business. That sort of arrogance led to trouble. Otto would have to be careful not to fall into the same trap. In truth, he didn't want all the responsibility he had. Spending his days reading books from the armory and practicing new spells would have suited him perfectly well. Only necessity kept him running all over hell and gone putting out fires.

He sighed and realized it was the only noise he could hear. The city was absolutely silent. No, the few ships tied up at the docks creaked as the waves pushed them back and forth. But there were no animals, no birds; the curse seemed to have killed them as well. Interesting. Was it possible to create a version of the spell that only affected humans? Otto filed the question away for later.

He drew the magic-repelling dagger with his left hand and

his mithril sword with his right. If only Graves could see him now. Off to have a sword fight with the last Arcane Lord. The good sergeant would no doubt laugh, as would Father, but Otto doubted Valtan had had as much sword training as him, which wasn't saying much.

Putting the distracting thoughts aside, he turned toward the royal palace. Unless he was mistaken, Valtan was supposed to have a tower there. If he couldn't find the old man there, he wasn't sure where he'd look next.

Otto made it halfway there before a strange shudder in the ether reached him. It was coming from the portal. Since he had no way to activate Markane's portal, Valtan must have done it.

Changing course, he ran for the portal.

E very step Valtan took felt like it might be his last. The Scroll had expanded to cover his neck, shoulders, and the left side of his face. It wouldn't be long before he couldn't control his body at all. If he hadn't made it to the portal by then, he had no hope. The pain, at least, had receded to the back of his mind. It wasn't that he didn't hurt anymore, he'd just gotten used to it enough that he could block it out.

You have no hope now. I can see your pathetic plan and even you must realize it won't work. Your body is tethered to this world. You can't leave it even as desperate as you are now.

He cursed Amet and kept staggering across the cobblestones. There was truth in the dead man's words, but he dared hope that leaping through the portal would sever the threads binding him here. And that's all it was, a wild, desperate hope. He had nothing else left.

The portal appeared not far ahead of him. Valtan rounded a

bend and found the plaza directly ahead. He was going to make it.

Just as he thought that, the Scroll reached his right leg and he fell to his knees. His control of that limb vanished then just as quickly returned. Not trusting his legs to hold him, Valtan crawled on.

Pathetic. Better for your dignity if you just accept your fate. At least you could do it on your feet.

Once more, Amet wasn't wrong. But Valtan had given up on his dignity the moment the Scroll attacked his body and he realized what was at stake. His pride meant nothing compared to stopping Amet from returning to the land of the living. If he had to drag himself with only one arm, he would.

Stubborn fool. At least my new body will recover quickly once I finish obliterating your mind.

Valtan had no strength left for banter. He crawled foot by miserable foot until at last he reached the portal. Reaching up he placed his hand on the cool mithril and concentrated.

Fresh pain wracked his tortured body, but he ignored it. He felt the Scroll spreading faster, but he ignored that as well. All that mattered was opening the portal.

At last he felt the magic he hadn't used in seven hundred years take hold. He peered up at the writhing green mists filling the opening. The netherworld had never looked so inviting. Now all he had to do was step through and hope he was right about the threads being severed.

"Valtan!"

He rolled over and stared in shock as Otto Shenk ran towards him. The boy had a mithril sword in one hand and a black dagger in the other.

Otto stopped a few feet away and stared. "What in heaven's name happened to you?"

O tto wasn't sure what to stare at first, the portal behind Valtan swirling with the sickly green energy of the netherworld, or Valtan himself. The Arcane Lord had clearly seen better days. Some strange second skin was growing over his body and his once-fine clothes had been blasted to shreds. Last of all he was crawling. What had happened to put the mightiest wizard in the world in such a state?

He shook his head. It didn't matter. "Where's the Scroll?"

Valtan's laugh was more of a wheezing cough. He reached up and touched his chest. "It's here."

Otto didn't understand. That weird second skin was the Scroll? "What did you do to it? Where's the secrets it contained?"

"It was a trap," Valtan said. "Amet planned to take over the body of a newly made Arcane Lord for himself. To be reborn. Instead he decided to take mine in revenge. You have to help me."

If Valtan was asking Otto for help, he must be truly desperate. More importantly, if what he said was true, his whole reason for coming here was gone. The secret of how to use the Immortality Engine was no more.

"Ignore this fool." A new voice spoke out of Valtan's mouth. The sound was the same, but the pronunciations were different. Otto had never heard an accent like it. It vaguely reminded him of the people of the City of Coins.

Then he understood. "Lord Sur?"

"I knew you were a clever boy," the new voice said. "I'm actually glad I didn't end up taking over your body. Help me subdue Valtan and I will make you my first apprentice. With my help, your transformation will be smooth and seamless. I can show you wonders of magic you can't begin to imagine."

Valtan shuddered and his original voice said, "Don't trust him. Amet will bring this world nothing but death and then he will spread it to other worlds. You told me once that all you wanted was peace. You will never know a moment of it if this monster is reborn."

Could he pass up a chance to learn at the right hand of the greatest wizard to ever live? The knowledge Lord Sur possessed made the secrets hidden in all the libraries in the world seem like nothing. But having seen the Amalgam of Souls, he couldn't deny the truth of Valtan's words. Anyone capable of creating such a horror couldn't be allowed to exist. Wolfric, Corina, his mother, none of them would be safe if Amet Sur succeeded.

"How do I sever the threads?" Otto asked.

Valtan's face registered relief before he shuddered again and his expression twisted into a sneer of contempt. "You would give up the power you've sought for all this time? From what this one and his lackey thought, I imagined you were made of sterner stuff."

"I've seen how you use your power and while I'm hardly the squeamish sort, I dislike killing for the sake of killing. Magic that consumes and corrupts souls—and I can't believe I'm about to say this—is probably better left forgotten." Otto thought for a moment then shrugged. "Or at least unused. I love the country I've built. The wizards living there are building good lives as are the ordinary people. I have no desire to see it turned into another Dead Lands."

"Idiot!" Valtan's body forced itself to its feet. "Humans are just a resource. Even the wizards are little better. They're all weaklings to be used and discarded as necessary for any given spell. You'll never rise above your limitations until you under-stand that simple truth. And I have no use for blind fools."

Valtan's hand shot out and a massive lightning bolt arced toward Otto's chest.

And fizzled a foot from his body. He hadn't even seen a targeting thread.

Otto let out a breath. Thank heaven for the dagger.

"Anti-mithril. Where did you find it? Never mind, it had to be Colt. The arrogant fool must have ignored my orders." Lord Sur shook Valtan's head and sighed. "Reliable associates are nearly impossible to come by."

Otto considered his own allies. They might not have been Arcane Lords, but at one time or another, they had each been indispensable to him. He wouldn't toss any of them aside lightly.

The ether shifted again and the ground rumbled under Otto's feet. He leapt right, narrowly avoiding an earthen spike that shot up under the spot where he'd been standing.

More spikes erupted from the ground, forcing him to run around the plaza, leaping and diving to avoid getting impaled. Just like mirrorshine, it seemed the dagger only protected him from direct attacks.

That was a problem as his chest was already getting tight from the unaccustomed exercise.

An explosion just to his left sent Otto flying. He landed hard but immediately rolled away, expecting a spike.

Instead, Lord Sur roared and grabbed his head.

"You weakened him," Valtan said. "Well done."

All Otto did was survive and he considered that a bit of a miracle.

"Once I'm through, sever the ethereal tentacle with the dagger. That will trap us and close the portal. I don't know if it means anything now, but I'm sorry for what happened to Garenland. Even my best intentions are worthless. The world is better off without Arcane Lords in it. Try to remember that."

Valtan gathered himself to leap then shuddered again. "No! I will not lose to a weakling and a coward."

Valtan's body thrashed back and forth as the two souls fought for control.

Otto scrambled to his feet and sprinted over before he could think better of it. A powerful front kick sent the madly struggling Valtan through the portal into the green haze.

The massive tendril of ether connecting Valtan to the portal hung only feet away. If he cut it, the portal network would power down, perhaps never to be activated again.

An agonizing scream came from the portal. Valtan, or likely Lord Sur, was trying to pull himself out using the tentacle.

Cursing the universe, Otto swung. There was no resistance as the construct parted. The green haze vanished along with Valtan's face.

Otto fell to his knees and blew out a sigh. "Say hello to Lord Karonin for me."

Not that anyone could hear him. He looked up at the portal, now truly powerless, and shook his head. Wolfric wasn't going to like this and the less said about the merchants' reactions the better. They would have to build high-quality roads and arrange patrols to dissuade bandits.

He smiled when he thought of all the work awaiting him as well as his quest to master all the magic Lord Karonin had gathered. One part of his quest may have ended, but much remained to be done.

EPILOGUE

After the battle with Valtan and Amet Sur, Otto became one with the ether and returned home. He never imagined the smell of clean clothes being so pleasant, but after the dead city, his closet in Franken Manor seemed like heaven.

He shrugged out of his filthy clothes and washed up. The cool water felt wonderful when it ran down his face. As he scrubbed the dirt, sweat, and fear from his body, Otto started to make plans. First he needed to talk to Wolfric. With the loss of the portals and his best chance—though he refused to believe it would be his only chance—to become an Arcane Lord, their future was far from guaranteed.

Otto dried his face and grinned. The only reason he wanted to become an Arcane Lord was so he could master magic beyond the power of a mortal man. An eternity with no real challenges would have been hell and it was a hell he suspected Valtan had known well. He would find another way to increase his power.

He still had the Immortality Engine, so extending his and

Wolfric's lives for as long as it took would be no problem. They could even offer an extended life span as a reward for those that served them loyally. That was quite a reward when you thought about it.

Someone knocked as he was buckling his sword back on. "Master? Are you okay?"

Of course, Corina would have sensed him returning. He'd left the girl here in case he returned and needed help. He crossed the room and unlocked the door. Corina looked at him with wide, worried eyes.

"I'm fine, though the mission was a total failure. Are the others here?"

"Axel's downstairs playing with Abby, Annamaria is taking a nap, and Hans is walking around the grounds pestering the guards. Want me to fetch them?"

"No, we'll collect Axel and Hans on the way. I need to go to the palace and talk with the emperor."

They walked down the hall toward the stairs. About halfway there Corina asked, "What happened?"

"The Scroll was a trap. It held the soul of Lord Sur. Had I succeeded in claiming it, I would have ended up dead and my body taken over by his soul. Instead, he took over Valtan. I sent both of them to the netherworld. There are officially no more Arcane Lords."

"At least until you become one."

He smiled at her confidence. Having seen what became of both Valtan and Amet Sur, not to mention the bitterness and hatred that defined Lord Karonin, he wasn't sure that was the right path for him anymore. There had to be another way to get what he wanted without becoming something he'd abhor.

Why was everything so complicated?

"I appreciate the vote of confidence. I'll be needing your help, so I hope I can count on you."

Her smile nearly split her face. "You know you can."

He did know it and that pleased him a great deal.

They found Axel lying on the floor and holding Abby over his head, swinging her around while making whooshing noises. He had his mottled-green scout uniform on, but his sword was slung on the back of a chair a safe distance away.

"You're wasted as a scout," Otto said. "Your future clearly lies in childcare. Maybe you and Cobb can start a daycare."

"You're a riot, little brother." He set Abby down on the carpet and stood. "I'm glad you're alive."

"Me too." They shook hands. "We're heading to the palace. Join us?"

Axel nodded and the maid on duty hurried over to collect Abby. As they made their way to the front door Axel said, "You know, it's probably not good that I spend more time playing with your daughter than you do."

"You're her uncle," Otto lied. "Feel free to play as much as you want."

"That's not what I meant." Axel pushed the door open and they climbed down the stairs.

Otto knew exactly what he meant and didn't want to discuss it any further. He stopped and extended his sight and voice. Otto quickly spotted Hans stalking around the grounds. No sign of the rest of the guys. That was okay, they weren't expecting a fight on the five-minute walk.

"Hans." The good sergeant jumped, making Otto smile. "We're heading to the palace. Meet us at the front gate."

Hans said something that Otto assumed was agreement. They stopped to wait at the end of the gravel path. Hans joined them after only a minute or two.

"How'd it go?" Hans asked.

"Less well than I'd hoped. I'll tell you as we walk."

Otto sighed as the guards opened the iron gate. He suspected he'd be telling this story a lot over the next few days.

O tto had slipped into the throne room without anyone noticing. He couldn't say he was surprised when he arrived at the palace and found the throne room packed with angry merchants. Someone must have discovered the portal had fully shut down. None of the war wizards would have said anything, but anyone watching would have seen it go dull and lifeless when Valtan got sucked into the netherworld.

From Wolfric's expression as he sat on the throne, he was getting tired of listening to them shout over each other. The blind fools were too worked up to notice his expression. Besides, it wasn't like the emperor could do anything about the portal. Wolfric had his talents, but magic wasn't one of them.

Beside Wolfric, Commander Borden looked ready to draw his sword and start hacking. Fortunately, he was far too disciplined to do something so stupid. Not that Otto didn't feel his pain. Dealing with these overstuffed idiots would test the patience of a saint.

Taking pity on his friend, Otto pushed away from the wall and strode up the central path to the throne. When the merchants noticed him, they all fell silent. A mixture of fear and hope mingled on their faces. If they were hoping Otto would provide them with an instantaneous solution, they were doomed to disappointment.

He bowed to Wolfric, turned, and said, "Valtan is dead and the portal with him. Until I can determine a way to switch them back on, you will all have to make do with overland and sea-born shipping, as will every other merchant in the empire."

The shouts resumed in greater volume. Otto raised his hands for silence. When he was ignored, he gathered a little ether in his fingertips and snapped them. A roar like the loudest thunder rolled through the throne room.

That shut them up.

"You can argue and complain all you want," Otto said. "But it changes nothing. The situation is what it is. When that changes, you will all be alerted."

"How long will it take to repair the portals?" a merchant with hollow cheeks and expensive gray robes asked.

"I don't know. It may not even be possible with my current skills." Otto stared around the room looking each merchant in the eye. "The current situation is difficult, but hardly as bad as being at war. You all survived that and you will survive this. Assuming you focus on your business instead of whining to the emperor."

Another man said, "By your leave, Majesty, may we be excused? Plans must be made."

"Of course," Wolfric said, all benevolence and smiles. "Know that the Crown will offer whatever help it can."

There were so many bows and nods of acknowledgement that it took nearly ten minutes to clear the throne room. Finally, only Otto, Wolfric, Borden, a squad of the palace guard, and Otto's companions remained.

"Heaven bless you, Otto. I was about to order them all hung for assaulting the imperial ears."

"My pleasure, Majesty." Otto smiled.

"Since you're here and alive and Valtan isn't, I assume you succeeded."

"In part. The threat from Markane is eliminated. But the

Scroll ended up being a trap. Another path will have to be found to my ultimate destination. On the plus side, at least we have little to worry us now. The main problems will be bandits and road maintenance."

Wolfric chuckled. "You just survived a battle with the last living Arcane Lord and you're already thinking how to overcome the empire's next challenges. Don't you ever stop to rest?"

Otto shrugged. "If the problems would kindly stop popping up, I'd be delighted to rest. That seems unlikely, so I do what I must."

"And the empire thanks you."

"Have you decided what to do about Eddred?" Otto asked.

"I think I'll take your suggestion and send him to the mithril mines. He might as well contribute something after all the trouble he caused."

"I volunteer to escort him north," Axel said. When everyone turned to look at him he added, "I promised Prince Uther that I would tell his father he died in battle. He might have been troublesome, but he was an honorable warrior in his own way. If it's not a problem, I'd like to honor his final request."

"If it's alright with the emperor," Otto said. "I have no objections. On your way, I'd like you to make a full survey of the roads and take notes on which sections need the most repair."

Axel grinned and shook his head. "Always making more work for me. No worries, I'll get it done."

Wolfric turned to Borden. "Take Commander Shenk to collect our prize prisoner. Otto and I need to have a private conversation."

While his brother, Borden, and the guards filed out, Otto turned to Hans and Corina. "Gives us a minute, guys."

Corina looked put out, but Hans led her out into the hall. At last it was just Wolfric and Otto.

"How does this impact our plans to rule the empire forever?" Wolfric asked.

"It does complicate them, but with the Immortality Engine still in our possession, I can extend our lives indefinitely. Condemned prisoners will provide more than enough life energy. No sense wasting it by hanging them."

"I suppose, but it does the people good to see villains brought to justice."

"If you want, I can have them walk out to the gallows as zombies and you can hang them then."

Wolfric pursed his lips. "Hanging them once they're already dead seems a bit distasteful. Well, we'll worry about that when the time comes. What will you do now?"

"The same thing I've been doing, search for new ways to become stronger, learn new magic, protect the empire. One avenue may have been cut off, but I have no intention of giving up."

Wolfric smiled. "The thought never crossed my mind. In fact, I can't imagine how the empire would survive if you did."

"Let's hope we never have to find out."

———

Otto emerged in the hidden tower and was surprised to find his master not in her mirror. It was well after midnight, but he doubted that would make a difference to someone living in the netherworld.

The perfectly clean stone chamber looked the same as ever. Not a single mote of dust drifted in the air. He'd like to know how she managed that, but in the grand scheme of things housekeeping spells were low on his priority list.

He'd chosen this time to visit so he wouldn't have to make any explanations for leaving again so soon after returning home. Everyone thought he was resting in his room.

Corina had returned to the warehouse, so there was no way she'd sense him leaving.

He shook his head. Who was he kidding? If he didn't feel like explaining where he'd gone, no one was apt to question him too closely.

At last the green glow filled the mirror and his master's face appeared. Her hair waved around her gaunt face like she was floating underwater. Her eyes had taken on a brighter glow than usual. If that meant anything, he didn't know what.

"This is a surprise. You seldom visit so late. I can't sense the Scroll, so I assume you failed." Her cold disappointment would have bothered him once. Now he just shrugged it off.

"The Scroll was a trap." He told her everything that happened. "Had Valtan not been available, I would have ended up the host for Amet Sur's soul."

She stared at him harder than usual. "You refused him? You refused to serve Lord Sur and destroyed him? Why? He could have taught you far more than I."

"He's insane. I don't know if he always was or if being stuck in a scroll in the middle of a desert broke his mind. Having seen the Amalgam of Souls he created, I'm inclined to think the former. No amount of knowledge is worth setting him loose on the world. Valtan was right about that at least."

He took a deep breath. His next question wouldn't be taken well.

"Did you know the Scroll was a trap?"

"You think I set you up to help my former mentor return

from the dead?" Her smile held no hint of amusement. "No, I had no idea. Amet kept his secrets close. A final chance like that he never would have spoken of lest his enemies find out."

Otto believed her. Lord Karonin's bitterness at not knowing sounded too honest to be fake. "Did he have enemies? I mean before Valtan betrayed you all. His soul is on your side of the mirror now, by the way. I hope that pleases you, Master."

"Amet had no enemies worth the name, but when you live for thousands of years, you become paranoid. As to Valtan, I hope the pig enjoys an eternity of misery and loneliness in this wretched place. It's no less than he deserves. What will you do now?"

"Resume the search. There's so much knowledge hidden in the world. I'll find another way to keep growing and increasing my power. The Immortality Engine assures that I have all the time I need. I hope I can count on your continued advice."

"It's not like I have anything else to do. And thank you for killing the pig." She grumbled that sentence so much he barely made out what she said. He further doubted he'd ever hear her offer him thanks for anything again.

"It was my pleasure, Master. Until we speak again." Otto bowed and became one with the ether.

Tomorrow he would resume his search for knowledge and power. He had once believed that becoming an Arcane Lord was the end of his search, but now he understood that there was never an end. The power offered by the ether was endless in its variety. He vowed to use it more wisely than his predecessors. Surely becoming the most powerful wizard ever didn't mean becoming a monster like Amet Sur.

Otto would find a way to reach the heights of magic and keep his soul intact. He swore it.

AUTHOR NOTE

And so we come tot he end of The Portal Wars Saga. I hope you've had as much fun reading it as I have writing it. If you'd like to join my newsletter to get weekly updates, new release announcements, and the like, you can find the link at https://www.jamesewisher.com You'll also get a free novella set in my Soul Force Saga world.

Thanks for reading and I'll see you next time,

James

ABOUT THE AUTHOR

James E. Wisher is a writer of science fiction and fantasy novels. He's been writing since high school and reading everything he could get his hands on for as long as he can remember.

To learn more:
www.jamesewisher.com
james@jamesewisher.com

Harvest of Souls

Disciples of the Horned One Omnibus

Chains of the Fallen Arc:

Dreaming in the Dark

On Blackened Wings

Chains of the Fallen Omnibus

The Complete Soul Force Saga Omnibus

The Aegis of Merlin:

The Impossible Wizard

The Awakening

The Chimera Jar

The Raven's Shadow

Escape From the Dragon Czar

Wrath of the Dragon Czar

The Four Nations Tournament

Death Incarnate

Atlantis Rising

Aegis of Merlin Omnibus Vol 1.

Aegis of Merlin Omnibus Vol 2.

The Complete Aegis of Merlin Omnibus

Other Fantasy Novels:

The Squire

Death and Honor Omnibus

The Rogue Star Series:

Children of Darkness

Children of the Void

Children of Junk

Rogue Star Omnibus Vol. 1

Children of the Black Ship